Sherlock Holmes

and

the Adventure of the Three Dragons

Sherlock Holmes

and

the Adventure of the Three Dragons

An original story by Luke Steven Fullenkamp.

1stbooks – rev. 3/24/00

ABOUT THE BOOK

The complete and utter destruction of London seems imminent. Holmes and Watson now face their greatest challenge ever. Never have they known an enemy with such a powerful and terrible technology at his disposal. The desperate quest is begun to stop the oriental master of the three dragons before he can carry out his lethal threat upon the innocent inhabitants of Holmes's and Watson's beloved home.

A beautiful and mysterious woman enters and soon captures Watson's heart. But what is her connection with the dragon master? And who is the strange oriental known as Guardian, and why is he looking for Sherlock Holmes?

Ancient, wonderful and terrifying sciences are rediscovered by an enemy so evil that the great detective cannot bring himself to call him by his proper name.

Can Holmes and Watson discover enough of his secrets in time to save their city and Queen? Will those who become their allies be able to help them stop the dragon master before he does the unspeakable? Will London be destroyed, and will a new China then rise from the ashes?

All is revealed in, *Sherlock Holmes and The Adventure of the Three Dragons*. It's Holmes and Watson at their best--during the worst--as you have never known them before.

For Sue and Adam and Paul,
with whom I share my love for adventure.

From the personal journal of Dr. Johnathan Watson:

August 03, 1881

In an effort to assure that time will not erode my complete recollection of the matter, and to guard against the possibility of any alterations in the sequence of events which I am about to reveal, it behooves me now to record this true and most astonishing account, that must surely be written before the passage of years brings the deaths of those who might confirm my story or otherwise refute its content. I speak of the passing of the Earl of Beaconsfield, Benjamin Disreali, a good friend and one of England's greatest Prime Ministers; who, were he here today, would surely agree to all I am about to pen. But since his death earlier this year, I have felt more and more compelled to commit all the facts of this astounding case to print.

To my knowledge, no part of these occurrences has as yet reached the public in any form. But should they ever be brought to light, let me say at this time that this record is as complete as is humanly possible.

Inasmuch as I have set myself to this task, I am determined to assure that the heroic work of the greatest detective who has ever lived should not pass away without proper acknowledgement. I speak, of course, of my most remarkable friend and associate, Sherlock Holmes.

Dr. Johnathan Watson

Sherlock Holmes
and
the Adventure of the Three Dragons

Chapter One

My story begins deep in the sewers of Paris. The small boat in which Holmes and I sat moved with relative ease down the narrow tunnel, lined with decaying, moss-covered walls that looked as though they had been there for a millennium. The air was cold and musty and seemed quite unfit for human consumption, although it did not appear to bother Holmes in the least. I squinted and blinked my eyes, trying as best I could to see but a few feet down the dark, forbidding passageway that lay before us. Looking over Holmes's shoulder--he being in the front--I glanced briefly at the lantern attached to the bow of our little craft, wondering if it had gone out. The pitiful small beam seemed of no significance in all the blackness. My friend, sensing my uneasiness, turned and smiled in a comforting manner. But even his steady face revealed the apprehension we both felt.

On occasion, we would pass the openings to other narrow tunnels leading off in all directions, giving one a feeling of disorientation in the confusing maze. But Holmes seemed to know exactly where he was going and slowed our little boat with his oar at every opening to the right, as though he were looking for some marker he had predetermined to find.

The bleak cavern seemed to go on forever and my mind--not so disciplined as my companion's--began to wander back to the events which brought us to this place and time.

The famed Ming treasures, on loan to France from the great nation of China, had been stolen from the Louvre museum in Paris. Having heard of my friend's remarkable talents, the French authorities had summoned Holmes and me to help them on this most difficult case, fearing the adverse repercussions the theft would have on their relations with the ancient country. The thief had been traced to the sewers and the capture would seem routine to an untrained eye. But after the dreadful mutilation of no less than six of the city's best policemen in the underground caverns, the case took on a new light.

Holmes was his usual brilliant self when going over all the evidence that had been collected by the locals, and had somehow deduced that the criminal could be captured by closing in on one large room in the sewer--the great conjunction room of several tunnels in the huge maze. Apparently he had discovered from an old print that a small room leading off the conjunction would remain dry even in the event of heavy rain. The thief would be sure to know this, as Holmes reasoned he was able to elude capture, thus indicating a familiarity with his surroundings.

After studying the remains of the unfortunate policemen, whose bodies you will remember were found mutilated, my companion had requested an elephant gun, which did little to assure my most uneasy stomach. For I knew it was not elephants we were after.

Holmes's plan seemed simple enough. He and I were to approach the great conjunction by boat, while the local enforcement traveled down to the large room on foot, by a higher route, free of water. We were to cut off his escape by the lower caverns, and they by the uppermost, dryer exits. The matter that unnerved me most was that the deceased policemen had been in boats when they met with their untimely deaths, and after hearing Holmes's theory as to how it came to pass, I must confess I did not look much forward to the trip.

The sudden sound of my companion's oar slowing us again brought me back to the damp, musty cavern.

"This is our entrance, Watson. We must now be ready for anything."

As we steered into the adjoining tunnel, the bottom of our boat scraped against an object, which upon examination proved to be the top of an iron gate, sunk in the water at the entrance. A series of small, sharp spikes protruded from the top and we took great care crossing over.

"An obstacle to keep us out?" I questioned.

"More, I think, an obstacle to keep something else in," Holmes answered.

We continued now, more cautious than ever. I had a strange feeling that my friend knew exactly who this criminal was, but he would not say, as it was his practice to withhold the final verdict until all the evidence was complete.

After a long row we heard the sound of gentle splashing in the water behind us and I turned quickly to see only the darkness of the musty cavern.

"If I don't miss my guess, Holmes, I'd say we're being followed."

"Quite right, Watson, for about the last quarter hour."

My companion missed little, and it was no small comfort to remember this fact.

"There, Watson, do you see it!"

I squinted in the poor light of the small lantern.

"See what, Holmes?"

"The thin wire stretched across our path, not much thicker than a spider's web."

He was right of course, and we used the oars to stop our craft only inches from the spot.

"Let's row back a short way, Watson, and see what we can make of this."

We paddled backward a small space and stilled ourselves again. My friend picked up one of several iron bars he had packed along and threw it with his usual accuracy at the place in question. This action caused a long metal spear to come streaking down from a hole in the ceiling, splashing into the water with great force, making the hair on my head to raise. Immediately there came the sound of thrashing from behind.

"Holmes," I reiterated, "someone is definitely following us."

"Someone or something," was his reply.

We continued our perilous journey, moving at a snail's pace. I kept us going with short strokes, while Holmes put his oar out in front and slightly under the surface to guard against any sunken danger.

About the time we started to catch our breath, my companion's oar hit home and a large rock came hurling from the roof, landing just in front of us. The resulting splash tossed our little boat backwards, nearly throwing Holmes and me into the foul water. But we managed to stay with it and I once again felt grateful to be in alliance with such a great mind.

"Have you noticed, Watson," Holmes spoke, having collected himself quickly, "how the traps we've come across so far have been designed more to sink us than to do us bodily harm?"

"Oh, I don't know about that," I disagreed. "That rock would not have done my head much good."

Holmes smiled. "That's very true, my friend. But while it might have disabled one man, it was not very likely to have struck both."

My companion's logic was indisputable as always, and I must confess I had to agree with his theory.

Continuing on in the same cautious manner as before, we kept our eyes wide, noticing everything. Having negotiated a rather sharp turn in the passageway, we spied a fairly bright light some feet ahead.

"Could that be our destination?" I whispered.

"Yes, Watson, I believe it is."

My heart began beating faster in anticipation of the confrontation I was sure would soon take place. Holmes was not always right about these matters, but he was rarely wrong; and everything we had encountered so far led me to believe that, in this instance, he was most definitely right.

As we drew closer to the end of the tunnel, I felt myself stiffen. Looking down, I could see the elephant gun Holmes had procured, nestled against his right leg--a practice he performed to stay in contact with a weapon without having to hold it. This told me the time had come. I was now ready for anything and even preferred confrontation to all this creeping around. In my haste, I started to paddle hard only a few yards from the opening, thinking of making an aggressive entrance, when my companion called to me, indicating the foolishness of my impulsive maneuver.

"No, Watson!"

Only an instant before, Holmes had spied the thin trip wire a few inches above the surface of the water. He struggled to paddle against me, and after a brief moment I joined his attempt to stop our small vessel before it was too late. The boat slowed, and barely touched the fine thread which stretched across our path as we came to a swift halt.

"Well, Holmes," I gasped, my breath short, "it would seem our luck is holding."

The words had no more than left my mouth, when two large, wooden beams came shooting out from either side of the tunnel, smashing our small boat to splinters, giving us a proper baptism in the dark, putrid water. My associate called out to me.

"Watson, are you all together?"

"All right, Holmes," was my reply as I groped for some hold on the slime-covered stone.

The incident had taken place in the opening just before the great conjunction room, and the light that came flooding in from the hole illuminated the tunnel fairly well. I looked towards Holmes, who was now along the side supporting himself on a small ledge that ran down both walls of the cavern. His eyes were fixed in an intense fashion towards the direction we had just traveled. I turned at once to survey the scene for myself, for his look was one I had come to know well. It said, danger is near. A moment later the horror came into our vision. Moving down the tunnel towards us, with hungry haste, was the largest crocodile I have ever seen. Words cannot describe the terror that welled up within me at the sight of this hellish apparition slinking out of the eternal night of the sewer.

I was frozen on the spot, and would have most surely perished there, had it not been for my companion's commanding voice calling instruction to me.

"Watson, swim this way! There is a gate at this entrance and it will protect us."

True to his unrelenting competence, Holmes had discovered another gate like the one we had encountered earlier, sunken a few inches below the water line, at the entrance to the great room. I swam with all my might and could see my friend waiting for me at the opening. We pushed over the gate

5

together, barely touching it in our haste to escape the hungry reptile.

Now inside the large room, I stood with my feet on the soft, mucky bottom while the water came to the top of my shoulders. I could see Holmes a few feet away, surveying the area with quick glances in every direction.

The great conjunction room was a sight, indeed. Well lit, with three torches on each of four walls, I could see the openings of several passageways like the one we had just left so quickly. Set at different levels of height, some spilled water into the collection pool where we stood, while others carried water away. A few of the higher tunnels were completely dry. The stone walls were dark and moldy, giving the room the look and feel of a tomb.

Holmes and I began to walk together towards the other side, as a dry landing with a set of stone stairs lay directly across the way. The stairs led up to an opening that looked more like a doorway than a tunnel--the doorway to the room my companion had spotted previously, in an old print of the sewers. We had taken but a few steps when a figure appeared suddenly in the opening.

"How nice of you to join me, Mr. Holmes." He paused. "And the good Dr. Watson as well, I see."

My eyes had grown accustomed to the darkness of the cavern and I had some trouble making out the form at first, but they finally focused and I now recognized the figure of a man; a vaguely familiar man.

"Thomas Bently." The words were heavy on my lips.

"<u>Sir</u> Thomas Bently," was his snide reply.

His title was self-issued, of course, as his typical conduct was hardly worthy of knighthood. "Thief-for-hire" would be more fitting. Although, I must confess, he was one of the best, not just in England, but the whole world. Holmes and I had encountered him on a few past cases and were directly responsible for his incarceration five years previous. It seemed Sir Thomas was involved in a plot to steal the jeweled crown of Britain. We thought him still in prison, but there he stood before us, as arrogant as ever.

"I see you have met one of my watchdogs, gentlemen." He was obviously enjoying himself. "I hope she did not inconvenience you."

"The she you refer to is a he," was my friend's reply.

"Why, Mr. Holmes," Bently laughed, "you are as clever as always. It's been years, gentlemen. How are you? I'm sure you've been quite busy, what with all the goings on in London these days."

He smiled momentarily, but his mood quickly soured.

"I have spent a lot of time thinking about our next meeting, gentlemen. As you well know, I've had a lot of idle time to spend--just thinking. When last we met, the advantage was yours. Now it would seem that the tables have been turned."

He suddenly became aware of his anger and changed his tone to that of mock friendliness.

"But I am forgetting my manners. You've just arrived and after all you are my guests."

Something was not right. Bently was a clever man and capable of any theft. But his defense system was too elaborate for a criminal mind of his caliber. Not to mention the gruesome nature of it all was directly against the man's character. In all the years we had followed Bently's sordid career, he had never once taken a single human life--until now.

The rather pudgy man began descending the stone stairway with the easy gait of an aristocrat. I could see quite clearly now and the signs of age were plain about him. A man in his late fifties--he looked much older--he was short and stocky, with a large stomach that had undoubtedly been caused by years of inactivity. He had a large nose and small ears that came straight out from either side of his head, giving his face, at first glance, a clown-like appearance.

"I should offer you good gentlemen some refreshments, but unfortunately, I must be leaving. With most of the local police down here looking for me, my going should be quite casual."

His words caused me to suddenly remember that the authorities were, indeed, on their way and it was most unsettling to realize that Bently was so aware of our plan. The very confident thief walked over to a wall adjacent to the stone landing and looked up at the very opening in which our reinforcements were due to arrive.

"It would be nice to entertain all of you, but then I was never one for large gatherings."

Reaching into his coat pocket, he momentarily retrieved a small metal cylinder about three or four inches in length and only about one inch in diameter. What appeared to be a small rod or stick protruded from one end. Smiling a charming smile, he pulled the stick from the end of the cylinder, tossed it up into the tunnel, and then pressed himself against the stone wall, cupping his hands tightly over his ears. Before I could make any sense of it, my companion grabbed me by the scruff of the neck and pulled my head under the water.

The resulting explosion was deafening, even while submerged, and the cavern room shook violently from the percussion. When we surfaced, bits of the ceiling were still falling all around us. The tunnel that was to give access to our reinforcements was spewing dust and debris from its damaged mouth.

Holmes, a man not easily shaken, broke in on the moment.

"Aren't we quite the showman!" he quipped. "You always did have a flare for the spectacular."

"Yes, indeed," Bently laughed, "and that is nothing, Mr. Holmes--a mere flicker of the candle compared to the breath of the dragons."

This statement confused me. What did he mean, I wondered. Probably the crocodile that tried to have us for his dinner, and could this mean there were more?

"Tell me, Bently," Holmes spoke as though visiting with the country vicar, "how came so clever a man to let himself be trapped by so common a police force?"

"Ah, that is a good question." The old thief now seemed less in a hurry. "Yes, I should have been away from here days ago, but unfortunately my reinforcements, like yours, were also detained. But perhaps it is all for the best. Perhaps this is how it should be."

A look of concern now came over him, and his voice became sad. "I cannot tell you how difficult this has been for me, gentlemen. Only recently have all the details become known to me."

I whispered to my friend, "Holmes, what is he babbling about?"

Before my associate could answer, Bently continued. "There is not much time left," he said, coming out of his daze. "It is time for me to go."

The sorry-looking thief walked over to the edge of the landing and began to pull on a rope that was fastened alongside. The other end, we discovered, was attached to a small boat, which emerged from a nearby tunnel. He stepped into it and stood, taking hold of a wooden bar that protruded from the old wall.

"And now good-bye, gentlemen. Do you see this curious device? I need only pull it down and all the gates that keep my watchdogs out of this pool will open."

I shuddered at the thought, for all through our conversation with Bently there had been strange sounds coming from several of the caverns. He now smiled again, but it was not the mocking smile of anger. It was a true smile.

"Some day, gentlemen, you will die," he paused, bleeding the moment of victory, "but today is not the day."

To my surprise, the aging criminal sat down in the boat and, taking an oar, began to paddle towards an exit.

"You must visit me in London, Mr. Holmes, Dr. Watson."

His weathered face became most serious. "You really must come. Our great city is in grave danger."

I was stunned to say the least. Not only was Bently sparing our lives, but he seemed to be asking our help as well. Holmes began to speak, as though he would venture another question when a new voice echoed in the room.

"Where have you been, Sir Thomas Bently?"

We all looked up to see three men standing in the mouth of a passageway located about ten feet above the landing. They were Orientals and stood as spectors in the dancing shadows that were cast by the unnatural light of the torches. Two of the men--one on either side of the center man--were dressed all in black and remained motionless, their arms folded in the Far Eastern manner. The center man, obviously the leader, was dressed as any common gentleman in England, and while his accent was evident, his mastery of the English language was accomplished. It was the center man who had spoken and who now continued.

"I have been waiting patiently for you for many days." His voice was steady and cold. "Have you been having second thoughts about our agreement? Did you decide the fee was too small?"

Bently was noticeably disturbed but struggled to act as though all was as it should be.

"I, ah . . . you can see I was unavoidably detained."

"Were you indeed," the Oriental replied. "Do you have the Ming treasures?"

"Yes! Yes, of course." Bently lifted a tarp in his boat and revealed two small crates. "They are here, and I'm sure our escape will be quite simple."

"I'm sure it will be," the dark figure told him.

The sinister spokesman now moved for the first time and motioned to his soldiers with little more than a nod of his head. The two men in black leaped onto the stone landing and reached into their shirt sleeves, pulling out a short knife with each hand.

Bently's expression turned to that of surrender, and after a brief moment of indecision he paddled over to the two henchmen. With no regard for the old gentleman, they stepped into the boat and pushed the poor fellow unceremoniously over the side.

Bently was in ill health. This I had noticed earlier, and I was relieved to see him surface, although his look was that of a man totally defeated.

"And now, gentlemen, it is I who will say good-bye."

The Oriental spoke from the security of his high tunnel.

"It is a pity we have no time to chat, Mr. Holmes. I have heard so much about you and was looking forward to taking tea with you one day. Oh well, my assistants will see that you are cared for."

The rude henchmen rowed toward the exit that Bently would have taken, but suddenly one of them turned and hurled an object at the lever on the wall behind. His throw was perfect and the wooden bar sunk in its place. I then heard the sound of metal grinding against stone and knew it was the gates to the water exits opening.

It seemed now that all was lost. Even Holmes, with all his cunning, could not have anticipated this. But when I glanced at him, as though to say farewell, I could scarcely believe my eyes. There he stood, shoulder-deep in the dark water, with the elephant gun from our lost boat leveled at the fleeing Orientals. Despite everything, he had somehow managed to hold onto it and had been concealing the weapon just below the surface of the water. The gun discharged with a loud report and the shot struck the top of the small boat, rocking it violently. The men in black were flung over the side and it was then that I noticed the many horrid reptiles moving in on three sides from the water-filled openings.

"Swim here, Holmes, Watson!"

The voice was that of Bently, beckoning us towards the landing. He was in the process of pulling himself from the murky water when another shot rang out. It came from the high tunnel opening in which the Orientals' leader stood. Bently had just gotten to his feet, but now winced in pain and slumped to the floor. I turned to see the cruel stranger holding a large pistol--smoke trailing from its barrel--aimed directly at my head. Before he could fire again, Holmes swung around and sent a booming volley of his own towards the merciless intruder. The man then disappeared into the seemingly endless darkness of the subterranean passageway.

All had happened in an instant, and I suddenly realized the crocs were closing in on us quickly.

"Let's not dawdle, Holmes," I blurted as we once again swam for our lives.

My companion was forced to drop the rifle, but we were able to reach the landing and pull ourselves to safety before the evil-looking reptiles could overtake us.

The two Oriental henchmen were not so lucky. They had been forced to retreat to a corner of the large room and had managed to pull themselves up onto a narrow stone ledge.

"Stay where you are!" Holmes called to the stranded men. "I'll try to retrieve the boat."

Surely these vipers were as dangerous as the crocodiles themselves, but my friend was never one to let any soul perish if he could prevent it--even men such as these. Holmes took the rope that Bently had attached to the boat, and began tying it to a piece of debris. As he did so, I noticed one of the Orientals reach into his shirt and retrieve a small dagger, like the ones they had threatened us with earlier. The man raised his arm to throw the knife, but paused a moment to steady himself on the narrow ledge. Spying his treachery, I leaped forward, pushing Holmes from the side, causing us both to topple in a haphazard fashion. The villain's throw narrowly missed my companion, but the action caused the ungrateful henchman to lose his balance. He fell forward, pulling his partner with him into the waiting jaws of no less than thirty hungry crocs. Their end came quickly as the water churned with the feeding, but the most remarkable thing of all is that neither man uttered a single sound during the entire episode.

Holmes looked to me with calm eyes. "My dear Watson, always there to guard my back."

The room was then still, but the silence was short-lived. A soft moan came from Bently, who was face down on the stone landing.

"He's still alive, Holmes!"

I went quickly to his side in the hope of using my medical skills to somehow save him, but one glance told me that the man was all but gone. Looking at my friend, I shook my head gently to let him know that the old thief would not be with us long.

Bently spoke softly, his breath labored. "Well, gentlemen, I told you I had to be going."

He winced once more in pain and opened his eyes wide, sensing the approach of death.

"I have made a most dreadful blunder, my friends." Bently struggled with the words. "To steal has been my life's work, but did you know that in all my years as a professional thief, I never once took a single life--until now, that is. I swear I didn't know it would come to this."

"Yes," answered Holmes. "I know you, Bently. That is why I did not fire on you earlier."

This, then, convinced me that the traps and crocodiles were surely the conception of some second party, probably the Oriental gentleman who undoubtedly hired the unfortunate Bently to procure the priceless Ming artifacts for him.

The dying man now clutched at Holmes's arm.

"London . . . our great London is in grave danger. The dragons will devour her and all within. The three dragons . . ." Bently felt himself slipping.

"Stop him," he uttered, pointing towards the exit where the mysterious Oriental had appeared.

"Stop him, or there shall be left . . . shall be left . . . not a stone upon a stone, nor a brick upon a brick."

These were his last words. I reached out to close his eyes and could see Holmes digesting the dead criminal's final message. There seemed to be no sense to his raving. I had been in many strange and exotic places with my dauntless companion, but never in all the years we had been together had I ever seen anything resembling a real dragon--much less one capable of devouring a city the size of London. But I could see from the look on Holmes's face that he was not so ready to dismiss the warning as the ramblings of an aging madman.

"Monsieur Holmes! Dr. Watson! Are you all right?"

The voice came from the doorway at the top of the stairs, and was that of Detective Rambeaux of the Paris police. Several regulars followed him as he quickly descended to the landing.

"I am sorry we are so late, but our passage was blocked and we were forced to find another route."

He walked over to us and looked around anxiously.

"Is this the criminal? Did you find the Ming treasures?"

"Yes to both questions," was Holmes's reply. "You will find them in that small boat."

Detective Rambeaux all but ran to the edge of the landing and was met there by a large crocodile just off to the side, its jagged, tooth-filled mouth wide open. Startled by the creature, he stepped backward, his mouth as gaping as the reptile's.

"What has happened here, Monsieurs?"

13

"It will take some time to explain," I volunteered. "You may wish to retrieve the boat with that rope."

The detective's men went to work securing the area, and we relaxed for the first time since we entered the great maze. Holmes was quite silent now and I knew full well what was on his mind. The words Bently had spoken were echoing all around us, as though his spirit were still hovering above, speaking them: ". . . not a stone upon a stone, nor a brick upon a brick."

Chapter Two

It was a mild evening in London, in the spring of 1879. The stars sparkled brilliantly in the heavens, while the sounds and sights of the city were most appealing to my native senses. The cabbies were calling for fares as their horses stepped in proper fashion. In the distance, I could hear the deep tones of Ben--Big Ben as he is now called--echo through the night air like a great watchman crying his hourly message that all is well.

At my side was Inspector Charles Whittington of Scotland Yard, who was joining me in a pleasant stroll to the apartment which I shared with my friend and associate, Sherlock Holmes. Actually, it was more than just a friendly jaunt. The inspector had been conferring with the French authorities and was quite concerned about the fate of the Ming artifacts that were on display in the London museum. Holmes and I had, ourselves, met with Charlie and discussed the entire matter at length. But the good inspector was a thorough man and had asked me to arrange another meeting with my friend, as he felt it necessary to review, once again, the events that had taken place in the Paris sewers a little more than a week previous.

Inspector Whittington was a fine-looking gentleman who always dressed as though he had an audience with the Queen; although that night Charlie had indeed met with Her Majesty, at a special celebration in honor of our Queen Victoria's birthday. His large chest strained the buttons of his silk vest, but it seemed to cause him no discomfort. His handsome, slender face jutted before him in regal fashion, making his entrance into any room a striking one.

I had attended the celebration myself, but Holmes had remained at home, exploring some bit of evidence he had discovered in the late Bently's apartment. As the inspector and I rounded the corner into Baker Street, we began to chat.

"You would think Mr. Holmes would have the time to attend Her Majesty's birthday. I mean, after all, he has always spoken as though he were her greatest admirer. One would assume he would at least show his face."

"Yes, well, I'm sure my friend would have done so, Inspector, if the work at hand were not so urgent."

I found myself making excuse for Holmes, although I, too, secretly wondered what could have been so important to keep him from this special occasion. His admiration for the Queen was boundless.

"You know, Charlie, Holmes always was a bit of the lone fish."

"That may be so, but I hope his absence has at least produced some lead in the Ming incident."

Charlie's sour mood was quite evident, so I decided to give him fair warning.

"I caution you, Inspector. My companion will not be bullied or intimidated. This you know yourself. He is an independent man and if you press him on this matter, he will do this investigation without you."

The inspector calmed himself and changed his tone.

"Yes, of course, Watson. I will be a perfect gentleman. It must have been the fireworks that fouled my mood. The Chinese have an affinity for noise that I simply cannot tolerate. It must be their way of punishing us for the Opium War. And the Queen, how noble she is. She smiled all through the entire evening, just to be sure that the Chinese delegates could see her gratitude. When I spoke with her briefly, it was evident that she was completely exhausted."

Charlie stopped his swift pace and paused on the walk to collect himself. He looked at me with new eyes now, and spoke frankly.

"John, you know how sensitive our relations are with China at this time. Nothing must happen to the Ming treasures here in London."

"Yes, I quite agree," was my reply. But my thoughts were more on Bently's last words and the fate of our city, than a collection of ancient home furnishings, whatever their importance in foreign relations.

We continued our walk in silence and finally reached the steps of the apartment. I remember how I so hoped that Holmes had at least tidied the sitting-room. My companion's mind was the most orderly and well-kept thinking machine known to man. His personal habits were second to none and he always smelled as though he'd just stepped from his bath. But when it came to keeping house, Holmes found it wasted motion. The study was a collection of papers, boxes, chemicals, and scientific instruments of every kind. One might sit in a chair only to find some strange stain left on one's trouser, from a substance that had no name.

Taking a deep breath, I opened the door to find the sitting-room cleaner than I had ever seen it.

"Here we are," I said, breathing a sigh of relief. No doubt Holmes had slipped the landlady a little something to satisfy my request.

"I'm sure he is in the study, Inspector. Let's go see what he may have found."

We walked through the sitting-room and into the narrow hallway which led to our study. The door was open, and as we entered it was obvious that my friend had done little to improve the room's appearance.

Holmes was seated at his desk, near a large window that looked out into the garden behind our home.

My companion was a striking figure as he brooded thoughtfully over his work. A handsome man in his evening attire--he was of average height and build, with dark brown hair that he always kept well trimmed. He had the reflexes of a mongoose and the steady hand of a surgeon. These latter attributes were not evident at first glance, of course, but there seemed to be an aura that surrounded him when he was absorbed in one of his projects.

I was about to announce our arrival when I observed my friend setting a match to a short fuse that protruded from the bottom of an object setting atop the desk. The object stood about six inches tall and looked very much like a small fountain pen.

Holmes then jumped from his chair and made for the stuffed sofa, when he spied us standing just inside the doorway.

"Dodge it, Watson!" was his call of warning to me. I knew it well and knew well what it meant; find the nearest hole and crawl in. I grabbed the inspector by his tight vest and pushed him backward through the doorway, landing on top of him as we plopped to the floor.

There was a loud hissing sound as the projectile ignited and rocketed through the open window of the study. But its flight was short-lived, for it landed on a large statue of General Cornwallis seated atop his horse, about fifty feet away from where we were. It exploded on impact and the detonation rattled the walls and windows. Needless to say, I was beside myself with my friend.

"Now you've done it, Holmes!" I shouted, storming into the room. "Mrs. Hudson will have us out in the street by morning!"

My companion stood from behind the security of the sofa and began walking towards the open window.

"Be at peace, Watson. Mrs. Hudson is in the country tending to her ailing sister. And believe me, she has been well paid to ignore any complaints that may result from this incident."

Holmes was not above a little bribery when it came to subduing our landlady, Mrs. Hudson. She would often complain about my associate's experiments and sometimes with good reason. But a wink from Holmes and a little something extra for her pocket would send her off tending to her ailing sister in the country. I really don't think she even had a sister. But whatever he paid her, it seemed to be enough to keep us in our apartment, after the deluge of complaints that were sure to come from the other tenants.

I joined him at the window and looked out into the garden. Through the clearing smoke, we could see that the tail and uppermost rear end of General Cornwallis's horse had been blown to dust. Holmes seemed quite pleased by the results.

"Well, Watson, it would seem I hit the wrong horse's ass. But I believe it's close enough to be considered successful."

I looked towards the doorway to see what might have become of the good Inspector Whittington. He was just peeking around the corner, his eyes straining to see if it was, indeed, safe to enter. Holmes welcomed him as though nothing had happened.

"Hello, Charlie, nice to see you again. Won't you join us?"

The inspector took a moment to compose himself and then walked in, still feeling a bit timid.

"I've quite had my fill of noise for one night, Holmes. I hope your experiment is over."

"Yes, Charlie," my friend chuckled, "I think I have all the information I need for right now. Please have a seat."

We made ourselves comfortable, moving the boxes of notes and equipment from the chairs while Holmes began to explain his reasons for all the bedlam.

"Here is a small sample of what appears to be gunpowder, Inspector. Guard it carefully. It is extremely sensitive to heat and percussion."

The inspector took the small parcel, wrapped in paper, and held it gingerly, as though it were an egg.

"If you bring it near the light, Charlie, you'll notice that the powder is very fine, like flour. But it's several times more volatile than anything I've ever seen. It looks enough like ordinary gunpowder, except for the greenish hue it takes on in bright light. I'm sure this substance was used to make the bomb that Bently had in the sewer, though I doubt he could have fashioned it himself. I've been working all evening trying to analyze its composition, but I must confess, with not much success. Perhaps your people will have more luck."

"What was that business with the firework all about?" the inspector questioned.

"I assembled that rocket based on some information I found in Bently's apartment."

Charlie blushed in embarrassment. His men had turned the place over several times and came up with nothing before Holmes had even been allowed in.

"I suppose I'll have to set a fire under some of my people. They must be getting a bit sloppy."

"Don't be so quick to think the worst about them, Charlie. I'm convinced the information and the sample were placed there sometime after your people left and before I arrived."

"What makes you think that, Holmes?" I asked.

"The items were hidden well enough and it took a bit of searching to unturn. But when I came upon them--tucked behind a loose brick in the fireplace--I noticed the small mark your men put on an article, to let the others know the spot's been checked. If the materials I discovered had been there earlier, your men would have found them."

The inspector looked puzzled.

"Why would someone want you to find these items intentionally?"

"If I knew that, Charlie," Holmes smiled, "I suppose the whole matter would be solved."

Just then the front bell rang.

"That must be Mr. Ling!"

The inspector rose and walked towards the doorway.

"I took the liberty of inviting someone from the Chinese delegation to join us, gentlemen. Hopefully you will be able to help me convince him that the Ming artifacts will be safe here in London."

Charlie left the room to get the door while Holmes and I walked over to the desk to inspect the smoldering hole left by the tiny rocket.

"What is it, Holmes? Why did you give Charlie that sample to analyze? I know you well enough to know that if you can't figure out what it is, Charlie's people most certainly won't fare much better."

"Yes, Watson, I must confess it is a ploy--a little something to keep Charlie busy while we look into other matters."

Our conversation was cut short by the arrival of the inspector and his guest.

"Gentlemen, I would like you to meet Mr. Chang Tow Ling."

The man stepped from the shadow of the doorway, and we came to recognize him as the mysterious Oriental leader from the Paris sewer. Instinctively I reached for the desk drawer that contained Holmes's pistol, but my companion caught me by the wrist and stilled my intention.

"It's a pleasure, Mr. Ling." Holmes spoke as though nothing were amiss.

"Mr. Ling," Charlie continued, "this is Dr. Johnathan Watson and, of course, you have heard of Mr. Sherlock Holmes."

"Yes, I have heard of both of you gentlemen." Ling spoke calmly. "As a matter of fact, we have met before. Very recently."

"How nice," the unwitting inspector said cheerfully. "Then you know that Mr. Ling is the assistant to the Chinese ambassador to Britain. Unfortunately, the ambassador was forced to return to China about six months ago, due to ill health. But Mr. Ling has carried on in his place and we are most grateful for his presence here in England."

We stepped forward to shake hands with our most unlikely guest. I remember his hand was cold and dry, and that the occasion was most distasteful to me. But I tried not to let on, while Holmes, in his usual way, was perfectly composed.

Charlie continued.

"Mr. Holmes and Dr. Watson will be working with us to protect the Ming treasures." The inspector tried to be convincing. "You may rest assured that nothing will happen to the artifacts so long as the Yard is on the case."

"I'm sure everything will be just fine." Ling smiled. "My trust in you is complete, Inspector Whittington."

The inspector smiled now and seemed very pleased by Mr. Ling's statement. If he had only known how close he stood to the greatest threat that endangered those artifacts it was his job to protect.

"I would like to stay and chat longer, gentlemen, but I really must be getting back to the castle." Ling spoke in the same calm voice as before. "Thank you for your time."

With that, he turned and walked out of the study. Charlie was hot on his heels and quick to continue his patronage of our guest.

"I quite understand," the inspector blurted as he followed, "Morlock Castle is a long way. You'll be all night getting home."

"Yes, it will be a long ride. Good-bye, Inspector Whittington--Mr. Holmes, Dr. Watson. You must come visit me at the castle. I have something to show you that I'm sure you'll find quite interesting."

"We surely will." Holmes looked him squarely in the eyes. "I'll be sure to make a point of it."

Ling stood motionless for a moment, his face blank. He then descended the steps of our apartment to where his coach was waiting. Charlie called after him as he boarded, "Thank you for your confidence in us, Mr. Ling!"

The coach moved off and the inspector stepped back into the sitting-room. He was rubbing his hands together, obviously quite satisfied with himself.

"Well, now, everything is right as rain. Let's go over the Paris incident again and see if there's anything we've missed."

"I think I've had enough for one night, Charlie." Holmes stretched as though quite fatigued. "Why don't you have your people get started on the sample analysis and we'll get together again soon."

"Oh--right you are, then." Charlie was too happy to argue. "I think I'll stop by the museum on my way home and make sure things are good there."

"A good idea, Inspector," I said, sensing that my friend was anxious to see him leave. "I'll stop by myself, first chance I get."

"Very good, then. Have a pleasant evening, gentlemen." The inspector stepped out onto the front landing.

"Shall I summon you a cab, Charlie?"

"No, thank you, Watson. It's such a delightful evening, I think I'll walk."

He left us then and strolled happily down Baker Street, disappearing into the calm evening.

"What were you thinking of, Holmes?" I asked. "Why didn't you tell Charlie about that Ling fellow?"

"Because, Watson, one does not go around accusing foreign diplomats without proof. But no matter. Are you up for a ride in the country?"

"What do you have in mind?"

22

"I've hired a coach to take us to Dover tonight."

"A coach! Oh, Holmes, couldn't we take the train? You know my back simply won't tolerate a ride on the rack. Ever since the Palmer case I haven't been able to get it straightened out."

"Sorry, Watson. There are no trains going our way tonight. I'll fill you in on the ride and we can catch a little sleep in between."

Now, if you've ever tried sleeping on a touring coach while traveling the country roads of England, you already know that the experience is not a pleasant one. But I reconciled myself to the trip and headed for my bedroom to change into my traveling attire.

"What's so important in Dover that we have to go this moment?"

"Morlock Castle, Watson. We're going to accept Mr. Ling's invitation."

"Why is the acting ambassador so far away from London?" I questioned, not happy about the unexpected journey. "Why aren't the Chinese here attending to protocol, instead of miles away in some old castle?"

"I checked into that, Watson. It seems Mr. Ling specifically requested Morlock Castle. Since the prime minister was anxious to please him, he granted the request. Ling travels back and forth with his people when necessary, but they keep mostly to themselves when at the castle."

"Well, I suppose you have a specific reason for wanting to go on such short notice?"

"I do, indeed, Watson." Holmes poked his head through my door as we'd been calling from room to room. "From everything I've seen and found so far, I feel strongly that time is of the essence."

Looking over at my companion I noticed his solemn expression and became convinced that the matter was more serious than I realized.

"Whatever you think, Holmes." I resolved to stop my complaining. "Give me another minute or two and I'll be ready."

Shortly after, the front bell rang. Holmes called to me from the sitting-room.

"Here's our ride, Watson!"

"Be there directly," was my reply.

I joined my associate at the front door and we went to the coach as the cabby tended to the horses.

"Nice night, gov'nors. It should be a chipper jaunt in the country," he chortled.

"I quite agree," I quipped as we carried our bags to the street. My spirits were lifted now as I began to feel the thrill of the hunt--a feeling that stimulated me and reminded me that life with my remarkable companion was always an adventure.

Opening the door of the coach, I inserted my head to examine our cramped traveling quarters. To my surprise, seated on the forward bench was the most beautiful woman I had ever seen. Holmes noticed her through the window and questioned the cabby.

"This is supposed to be a private fare, sir. You appear to have another customer."

"I thought you knew, gov'nor. The lady told me she'd made the arrangements this morning. Should I ask her to step out?"

Holmes paused for a moment. "No, that won't be necessary. Let's be off."

"Right you are, sir."

We joined our mysterious traveling companion and settled in for the long journey.

"Please forgive my small lie to the cabby, gentlemen." The lovely woman spoke softly. "I was desperate for passage to Dover and when I learned your coach was going there, it seemed expedient to make my way on board."

"You have business in Dover, then?" Holmes seemed truly interested.

"Well, not exactly. My brother has written me and requested that I attend the funeral of a dear friend of the family. I did not know the man myself, but apparently he was an associate of my father."

"Indeed, and who is your father?" Holmes questioned.

24

The woman blushed now in a most charming fashion. She was a radiant girl with milky, white skin--though her hair was as dark as any I had ever seen. She appeared to be in her late twenties and was dressed like a proper lady.

"Oh, please forgive me for not introducing myself, gentlemen. My name is Emily Morgan Cantaville, of the London Cantavilles. My father was Windslow Emmit Cantaville."

"Oh, yes, Whinny!" I interjected. "I knew your father some years ago. A very fine gentleman. I was deeply saddened by the report of his passing."

"Thank you, Dr. Watson, he really was very special to me. You may not remember, but we met once many years ago at a party given by my father."

I replied enthusiastically. "Now that you mention it, Miss Cantaville, I believe I do remember the occasion. We were somewhat younger then."

Holmes seemed to become curious at that moment and entered the conversation.

"Your family line is very old, madam. The Cantaville name goes back several centuries."

"Yes, we're very established, thanks to the Cantaville men."

I suddenly noticed that my associate was eyeing our pleasant guest in the particular way he does when seeking information for a case. His look was dreamy and I was quite certain he had already deduced how accurate the woman's statements were, what part of London she was from, and probably the entire menu of her last meal.

Needless to say, I was not pleased with my friend's manner and made my feelings known to him by a sharp blow to his left ankle with my boot. My companion's reaction was a faint grin, as he seemed mildly amused by my attention to Miss Cantaville.

We conversed all through the night, and after a while even Holmes seemed to relax and enjoy our pleasant company. The ride that would normally have been nothing short of torture became a picnic, and I could hardly believe it when the cabby called for our last rest stop before Dover.

"Well, gentlemen, I must say good-bye to you here."

25

My friend and I were sorry to say farewell to our lovely guest.

"My brother is sending a carriage to meet me here, but I must say I have enjoyed your company. We must visit again some day. Thank you for allowing me to share your coach."

"The pleasure was ours, madam." Holmes was polite but reserved. "Please say hello to your brother for me."

"Yes, I will," she replied, and then glanced downward as though suddenly distant. "Thank you again, gentlemen. I will not soon forget your kindness."

The cabby then called us aboard and we were off on the last leg of our journey. Morning arrived and first light peeked through the windows. We sat silent for a long while, but then I started to notice the rough roads that had seemed so smooth before the lovely woman departed.

"My back is feeling every pebble, Holmes; funny I hadn't noticed it earlier."

"Yes," my friend mused, "you were quite occupied before."

"Tell me, Holmes," I questioned, "why did you ask Miss Cantaville to say hello to her brother for you? Do you know him?"

"Actually, Watson, we've never met. But I was involved in a case that concerned him once."

I was curious about the circumstances of the case, but Holmes seemed reluctant to talk about it. I left it alone, assuming he would elaborate on the particulars when he was ready.

We were suddenly jolted by a large rock in the road and I moaned from the agony in my back.

"Take heart, Watson, we'll be at our lodging soon and a long afternoon's nap will do us both good. I want to be fresh for our visit to Morlock Castle tonight."

"So we're going to the castle this evening? I can't help but wonder what kind of reception will await us."

"I wouldn't worry too much about it, Watson. If I have my way, no one will even know we've come."

"Oh, I see! More creeping around in the dark. Why couldn't we just use the front door like everyone else?"

I laughed a hearty laugh now and my companion joined in.

"Yes, that would be a good one, Watson. Go right to the front door and say, 'Hello, Mr. Ling. Would you mind if we took a peek around?'"

"Yes, indeed," I chimed in, "we won't take but a moment of your time. Just show us the dragons and we'll be off."

My companion chuckled a bit longer but then lost the mood.

"Oh, yes, the dragons. The time was passing so pleasantly I almost forgot about them."

"Come now, Holmes, you really don't believe all that rubbish about dragons."

"I do, indeed, Watson, and I have a bad feeling that their bite is worse than their bark."

Holmes then revealed to me his theory of the dragons, and it was a gruesome one at that. But after he explained to me all the evidence on which he had based his assumption, my eyes were opened for the first time to the reality that Bently's warning was more than just the ravings of a sorrowful, aging thief.

When we finally reached our lodging, we plopped exhausted into our beds and slept away the afternoon and most of the early evening. Our encounter with the beautiful Miss Cantaville remained with me, as I dreamed of her glowing face and soft-spoken manner. I could hear her speaking, when suddenly another voice aroused me from my slumber.

"What do you say, Watson? We've time for a meal and a chat if we knock up now."

The voice was that of my companion, who had risen and dressed before me. I dressed myself quickly and joined him in a walk down to the dining room. As we finished our meal, Holmes looked at me in a way not typical of his usual countenance.

"You know, Watson, this little search is one that I could easily handle myself. You may wish to remain here until I return and then . . . ."

"What are you saying, Holmes? Wild horses couldn't keep me away from this one. Besides, if I weren't there, who would guard your back?"

"I was hoping you would say so, my friend. Nevertheless, this could be a sticky one."

We sipped our drinks and planned our assault on the castle. As I listened to Holmes, his voice became a dull drone and my mind returned to his theory of the dragons.

"What do you think, Watson?"

"What? I'm sorry, Holmes. My mind's still a bit foggy from the nap."

"It's quite all right, my friend. I'm still feeling a bit fuzzy myself."

We went back to our room and prepared a few things for the evening raid. My companion was more quiet than usual and I questioned him about it

"This one really has you worried, doesn't it?"

"Yes, Watson. In all my years of detective work, I've never encountered anything like it."

Holmes reached into our travel case and retrieved my pistol.

"Here's Mildred." He smirked.

Mildred is the handgun that I have carried ever since my first case with Holmes. He always thought it silly to name a weapon, but it generally amused him. Mildred was named for a woman I used to know who tended bar in a small tavern that was once my stomping ground before I settled down to a more respectable existence. She was a short woman with a hefty build and a loud mouth. This describes my pistol to a T.

Although my companion's weapon had no such title, his mastery of its feel and use was one honed and sharpened by hours of practice. The missing ears of General Cornwallis's horse in our garden were proof enough of that.

We finished gathering the materials, and it was well after midnight when we set off for Morlock Castle. We rode on horseback for about an hour and then left our mounts to complete the journey on foot. After a short hike, the dark silhouette of the old castle became visible to us.

Located near the sea, the structure was quite large and dated back to at least Henry VIII. Its high towers stood like giant ghosts in the moonlight, overlooking a large pond that had once been part of a moat, which entirely surrounded the ancient relic at one time. The pond was all that remained of the moat, and a stone bridge spanned its width, leading to the front gate. The castle was once used as a vacation spot by reigning monarchs, but had fallen into disrepair and had sat empty for several years; until just recently when the Chinese delegation had requested its use and insisted upon doing all the renovation themselves.

"I believe the back door would be more appropriate this evening, Watson."

"Right you are, Holmes."

We made our way around to the rear of the castle, near the sea, and decided to attempt entry through a small window which led into the first-floor kitchen. It was quite dark within, but once inside we felt our way to the exit which opened into a large hallway. Dimly lit by candlelight, it stretched about sixty feet down the way, with the doors to several other rooms adjoining it. These were the servants' quarters.

We knew from some information Holmes had obtained that a wide staircase at the end of the hall ascended to the throne room, which had once been used for affairs of state and large gatherings by the monarchy of old. It encompassed the second story almost entirely, and its ceiling stood a majestic forty feet above the floor, supported by several thick, stone pillars.

When we reached the top of the staircase, our first view was a most spectacular one. The room lay before us, its marble floors cleaned and polished. Bright, colorful banners hung from many of the columns, and a large, ornate throne had been restored to its original, historical place. Behind the throne was an immense curtain that spanned the distance from ceiling to floor and wall to wall. Three large, winged dragons were painted on its surface--their fierce-looking heads pointing down towards the great chair that sat upon a pedestal of sorts. Beside the pedestal was a Chinese gong that bore the same symbols of the dragons as those on the curtain. It was about four feet in diameter and was suspended by ropes from a metal stand.

We stood for what seemed an eternity, scanning the room in awe of the amazing spectacle.

"Well, Holmes," I whispered, feeling quite ill at ease, "now that we're here, what exactly are we looking for?"

"I'm not completely sure, Watson, but I think we'll know when we find it."

We ventured a few steps further within and then noticed a rather large table located towards the center of the curious room. The table appeared round in shape and was covered by a great silk sheet, or blanket, which draped all the way to the floor. The top of the table bulged upward in several spots as though something were concealed under the silken cloak.

"Let's see what we can make of this, Watson."

Approaching the table with some caution, my companion inspected it thoroughly and then slowly pulled the cloth from its placing. There, to our surprise, sprawled across the table's surface, in perfect scale, was a precise model of our beloved city of London. The detail was magnificent. It was obvious that meticulous care had been taken to reproduce the city to the last cobblestone. Holmes and I looked at each other in puzzlement. What could this mean?

"I'm very pleased that you have accepted my invitation, gentlemen."

We spun around to see that the words had been spoken by the mysterious Mr. Ling, who was standing near the throne--his face bright with satisfaction. But this shock was nothing compared to the sight of the lovely Miss Cantaville standing at his side.

"Emily, are you all right?" I questioned, not knowing what to make of it.

"You have met Miss Cantaville, of course," Ling continued. "She has been kind enough to keep a watchful eye on you good gentlemen for me."

Holmes seemed totally oblivious to the whole situation and acted as though he had expected all. I, on the other hand, was most distraught and made no bones about making my feelings known.

"It would seem you have found yourself a proper Judas," I remarked as my eyes burned holes in the beautiful traitor.

At that, she lowered her head as though thoroughly ashamed.

"Now, now, my dear," Ling's voice was that of mock compassion, "you must not let Dr. Watson upset you. You have done your work well and I shall see that you are properly paid for it."

Emily's head sank a little lower now and she tried to move away from her tormentor, but he restrained her by roughly taking hold of her arm. It was then that Holmes reacted to the situation for the first time.

"That is no way to treat a lady, Mr. Ling!"

My companion's voice was so commanding that he released her at once, and I was myself surprised by Holmes's almost rage-like response. But Ling just smiled benignly and continued his speech.

"Yes, gentlemen, Miss Cantaville can surely use the money. You see, the Cantavilles are quite destitute these days."

Ling spoke in the same cold voice as before.

"It seems the lady's brother was a very poor manager, indeed. The Cantaville family is quite penniless. Isn't that right, my dear?"

The woman spoke not a word.

"Why don't you tell them how your brother squandered the family fortune on bad investments and then, when all was gone, took his own life, leaving you quite out in the cold?"

She remained silent, but Ling was ready to tell all.

"So very unfortunate. What does a woman do when she has no means of support?" He paused as she began to cry. "I have heard that some women turn to prostitution. In the higher circles of society, I am told the wages are quite good."

It seemed that the merciless Mr. Ling was purposefully shaming the unfortunate Miss Cantaville before us. I didn't know if he was just toying with her or if there was some reason for his verbal flogging, but the affect it had on my companion was a definite one.

"You have convinced me, sir," Holmes's tone revealed his anger, "that you are a cad and a scoundrel. And if you care to give me the proper satisfaction, I should enjoy thrashing you soundly for your poor manner."

I thought it expedient at this moment to introduce the callous Mr. Ling to Mildred, my pistol. But my hand had no more than opened one button on my riding coat, when several of Ling's soldiers stepped out of the shadows from where they had been standing guard in silence. They encircled us quickly, while one came forward and relieved us of our weapons.

"I would like to accommodate you, Mr. Holmes, but there are more urgent matters to be dealt with."

Ling spoke a command in his native tongue which caused a guard to move to his side in obedience.

"See that Miss Cantaville is paid in accordance with our agreement and given passage back to Dover."

It was obvious to us that he had spoken his order in English so that we could understand.

"You have been of great assistance to me, my dear. Perhaps we can do business again in the future."

Emily had stopped crying now and turned quickly to leave. As the henchman escorted her towards the stairway, she paused for a moment and turned as though she would speak. Her face looked hardened, and she held herself erect now, as if to display no regret for her actions. But without a word she left the room, and we turned our attentions back to our unpleasant captor.

"Do you like my rendition of your London, gentlemen?" Ling strolled casually over to the large table. "I think it is marvelous. Great care was taken to assure that nothing was left out. Come and see for yourself."

I looked at my companion. "What do you think, Holmes?"

"Well, I suppose we should, Watson." Holmes's manner was matter-of-fact. "After all, they seem to have gone to a lot of trouble for our sake."

We joined Ling at the table and examined the scale replica with all its details. Even the most insignificant structure appeared to be represented. I had to admit, it really was astounding.

"What do you think, gentlemen?" Ling prompted.

"Well, I must say," Holmes answered, "it seems quite complete."

"Wonderful, I'm glad you think so." Ling gloated. "Now, come over here and stand by me. There is something you really must see."

We walked over to the throne where Ling seated himself, and had no more than arrived when the Oriental clapped his hands, causing the guards to disappear.

"Now, gentlemen, the moment is at hand. Behold the first dragon!"

Ling clapped his hands once more and we heard a loud hissing sound that emanated from a far corner of the grand room. I stood puzzled, not knowing what to make of it. But Holmes deduced the matter quickly and covered his eyes with his arm-- stepping in front of me to block my view of the miniature city.

"Watson, your eyes!"

He had spotted Ling doing the same an instant earlier, and realized the danger.

The tiny projectile struck its mark and exploded with a sharp report, sending forth a bright flash of light--the heat from which we could feel even at our substantial distance. My friend lowered his arm and stepped to my side, revealing to me the damage that had been done by the small firework.

To my horror, about one-third of the miniature London lay in ruin, while much of the rest of it burned.

"And now," Ling spoke again, "behold the second dragon!"

He clapped his hands, twice this time, and another loud hissing sound was heard coming from a different corner of the room. I was ready for it now and shielded my eyes quickly to protect them from the flash. The second rocket landed with the same result as the first, leaving another third of the city in ruin, while what remained burned with a hot flame.

"It would hardly seem necessary at this point, gentlemen, but let us finish what we have started."

The dark Oriental clapped his hands thrice and called out in a triumphant tone, "Behold the third dragon!"

The entire sequence was repeated, leaving nothing on the table but a mound of burning debris. The painstaking miniature, at which we had marveled earlier, had been reduced to a smoldering pile of ashes in a matter of moments.

Holmes stood calmly, giving not the slightest hint of emotion, while I, on the other hand, could not restrain myself.

"If this is your idea of levity, man, I find it most disgusting!"

33

A wide smile faded from Ling's face as he digested my reaction.

"I assure you, Dr. Watson, I am quite serious."

He then stood from his regal chair and stepped down from the pedestal.

"Come this way." His tone was somber. "There is one more demonstration you must witness."

We were led by Ling's guards to a door which opened onto an impressive balcony off the throne room. It was located towards the rear of the castle and gave us a beautiful view of the moon over the English Channel.

"Look out into the sea." Ling pointed to a small clump of rocks about fifty yards offshore. "Do you see it, gentlemen?"

Holmes nodded in recognition. Ling then motioned to one of his men, who called out in a high-pitched shout. A moment later, we saw what looked like a flare go streaking off from the roof of the castle. It climbed to a tremendous height and then exploded with a bright orange light.

"Watch the rocks, gentlemen, and you will find my meaning."

We stood patiently for a short time gazing out over the peaceful channel, when suddenly a bright line of red light appeared in the heavens. It seemed to be traveling at a substantial rate of speed and moved in a great arc towards us. The projectile crashed onto the clump of rocks, but while its impact was hard, the resulting explosion was a small one.

"The rocket you have just seen," Ling explained, "was four feet in height. It traveled a distance of ten miles and hit its mark precisely. Had I filled it with powder instead of clay, we would all be dead now and this great castle would be level with the ground. If you multiply my example by ten, you will know the extent of my power."

Ling's meaning was a clear one. He made it evident that he was capable of sending a rocket ten times the size and strength of this one, ten times the distance, with lethal accuracy.

"What do you think of my dragons, gentlemen? Are they not impressive?" Ling's mood was cheerful again. "The

34

guidance machine for this rocket is one of my own design. It is so small that it will fit comfortably in the tip of the firework."

The dark Oriental became noticeably excited, and continued his boasting as though unable to contain his pride.

"We Chinese have been building rockets for almost a thousand years, but even my ancestors never dreamed of such a weapon as this."

Ling paused now, as he had perceived himself becoming careless in his enthusiasm. With a more reserved tone, he continued his speech, choosing his words with thoughtful discrimination.

"Yes, it is I who gave the dragons their eyes to see and wings to fly." He paused again, looking Holmes dead in the face. "But I must confess that the dragons' fire is not of my own creation. You see, it was made a gift to me by a mutual acquaintance of ours, Mr. Holmes."

My companion now squinted his eyes in puzzlement. I remember it well for it was rare occasion, indeed, when Holmes was caught off guard. But a moment later his brow lifted, and was replaced by his usual countenance of quiet understanding. He then whispered, under his breath, a name which I had heard him use only a few times before this matter.

"Mephistopheles."

The name is, of course, the one given to the devil in the old Faust legend. But Holmes used it to describe a man who he was convinced was responsible for the majority of all crime and evil which took place in Europe. He claimed that this man was an Englishman who was bent upon destroying all good. But whenever I questioned him about it, he would never tell me the man's proper name or even what he looked like. He would only say that great care must be taken; for Holmes truly believed that this human monster was constantly seeking to destroy him for his personal endeavors against crime. And the only name by which he ever called him was Mephistopheles.

My friend now suddenly came alive, and he pressed Ling to get to the heart of the matter.

"Just what is it that you hope to gain from all this madness, Mr. Ling?"

35

"What do I hope to gain, Mr. Holmes? All right, I'll tell you plainly. The British government will relinquish unto me all of the Ming artifacts in the London Museum--those in the private collection of Mr. Richard Pattonsworth, and those on loan to the Louvre Museum in Paris."

"Is that all!" I said sarcastically.

"Not quite, Dr. Watson. In addition to this, your government will pay to me the sum of ten million pounds sterling."

"Ten million pounds!" I gasped. "You truly are mad, sir, if you think Her Majesty would even remotely consider such a ridiculous demand."

"Tell me, Mr. Ling," Holmes inquired, "do you do this on behalf of your government or is this a personal threat?"

At this our grave captor became enraged.

"Do you think me a pawn so easily used! Do you think me ordered around by the fools who call themselves rulers! It is I who will rule China and most of the rest of the world as well. For I am China, and I shall rule by my might--by the might of my dragons?"

"And if your demands are met," Holmes interjected, unaffected by the Oriental's ravings, "you will spare London from this destruction?"

"Yes, of course," Ling replied, making an effort to calm himself, "despite what you may think of me, Mr. Holmes, I am a man of honor."

"Are you, indeed, Mr. Ling?" My companion now had a look of fire in his eyes. "A man of honor, you say. Is that why you were so cordial with Miss Cantaville? Is that your reason for plotting the unspeakable destruction of over a million innocent men, women and children? Did you know that blackmail is one of the most cowardly acts a man can commit! You, Mr. Ling, are surely akin to the spineless creatures that crawl through the darkest regions of this ocean of life."

Holmes's taunting struck a nerve, causing Ling to become irritated once more.

"Is that so, Mr. Holmes?"

Ling turned and spoke Chinese to one of his soldiers, who promptly left us.

"You mentioned earlier that thrashing me would give you satisfaction. Perhaps I will give you the opportunity, and perhaps you will discover that doing so will not be a simple matter."

The soldier returned presently carrying two wooden poles about five feet in length. He delivered them to his master who, having tested their weight with his hands, extended both to my associate for his choosing.

"Are you familiar with the martial arts, Mr. Holmes? Have you ever seen what one of these can do to a man's head?"

Impatient for a reaction, Ling tossed one of the rods to my companion, who caught it an instant before it struck him.

"Very good, Mr. Holmes."

"I can't say I'm well acquainted with your martial arts," my friend spoke confidently, "but this doesn't seem much different than a quarter staff."

"I'm glad you approve. Then you will have no objection to sparring with me a bit."

Ling walked to the edge of the balcony, and with one swift stroke shattered a large flower pot that was setting on the railing.

"Shall we begin, then?" The Oriental was, himself, a confident man.

"I'll act as your second, Holmes," I said, helping my associate off with his riding jacket.

I knew that Holmes had intentionally provoked Ling, as it was his usual strategy to create some type of diversion whenever the odds were stacked against us.

I whispered into his ear, "Just say the word and we'll make for the nearest exit."

"Right you are." Holmes spoke aloud as he addressed Ling. "What are the rules?"

"There is only one rule, Mr. Holmes." Ling's face became taut. "Try to stay alive."

With that the sinister man charged my companion. But Holmes was ready and sidestepped Ling, giving him a sound shot on his behind as he passed. This infuriated the Oriental, who charged once more, this time striking at Holmes's head with a forward thrust. My companion blocked the blow and parried--

spinning around swiftly, striking Ling on his right shoulder. He winced in pain and backed away, startled at my associate's speed and skill. A few of the many henchmen that stood around us moved forward as though to intervene. But Ling motioned them back, his pride more wounded than his arm.

"You have the reflexes of a snake, Mr. Holmes." Ling smiled, collecting himself. "It would seem I have been taking you too lightly."

He then sprang forward, attacking my companion with new vigor. Holmes now blocked and dodged several more thrusts, but soon found himself with his back against the castle wall. Feeling the stone behind him he moved forward, striking out fiercely, putting his feisty opponent back on the defensive. I was sure that Holmes was about to make his move, so that we could attempt our escape, when Ling suddenly motioned to one of his soldiers. The henchman came at my companion from behind and kicked his legs out from under him. Before I could call a warning, Holmes was on the floor.

"And you call yourself a man of honor," I snapped, quite disgusted by the Oriental's treachery.

"Yes, Dr. Watson. But the word has different meanings for different people."

Ling now stepped over my friend who was still stunned from the fall. It seemed to me that he could have ended things very quickly, but he paused as though waiting for Holmes to collect himself.

"I may be a tart, but you, sir, are dirt!"

We all looked up to see Miss Cantaville standing in the doorway of the balcony. She was holding a large pistol, which seemed ridiculously out of proportion for her petite, feminine hands. Closing her eyes, she began squeezing off one round after another, sending Ling and his soldiers fleeing in all directions. Holmes and I deduced that we were the beneficiaries of this rescue attempt, but the aggressive woman's random firing caused us to join the villains in seeking cover. We dashed about like cornered mice, looking very much like proper fools to each other. After the gun emptied, we peeked out from behind the stone bench we had used for protection to see Miss Cantaville retrieving a second pistol from her purse.

"Make a go for it, gents. I'll hold them off as long as I can."

She then opened fire once more as we made our way to the doorway crawling on all fours. Once there, Holmes and I grabbed the brave woman by her arms and sped off like fleeing bandits for the stairway that led to the first floor. While we ran, Emily continued her barrage as she was still facing the balcony.

She soon emptied the weapon and then dropped it to the floor, struggling to release herself from our grasp.

"Let me be, gentlemen! Save yourselves!"

"Sorry, madam," was my breathless reply, "but that really wouldn't do--chivalry and all that, you know."

As we approached the stairway, we spied several of Ling's men ascending towards us. They gave chase, forcing us to retreat to a large window located towards the front of the room. Looking out, we saw the quiet pond that lay before the castle--a good forty feet below us.

"Escort Miss Cantaville out, Watson. I'll be along directly."

"Right you are, Holmes," was my reply as I grabbed the unsuspecting woman around her waist and jumped to the security of the water.

"Oh, no!"

Emily screamed all the way, but held on tightly, not wanting to jeopardize our landing.

Holmes, who was still standing in the window, tore the curtains from their fastenings and hurled them at our relentless pursuers, blanketing them with the tapestry. Catching sight of Ling at the far side of the room, he called a final message.

"We shall meet again, Mr. Ling! And I assure you, I will be looking forward to the moment."

With that, Holmes leapt to the pond, swimming over to where Emily and I were waiting for him.

"Let's be off," I spoke as we fled once more, making for the cover of the woods.

We reached the trees and had gone only a short distance when my companion slowed the pace.

"I think we can rest a bit now, Watson. I'm quite confident no one is following us."

"What do you mean, Mr. Holmes?" Emily spoke, still quite visibly shaken. "We're not out of reach yet."

Holmes looked at her now with soft, reassuring eyes.

"Ling has allowed us to escape. It was his plan all along. We, madam, are to be his messengers to the Queen. I'm sure it explains the ease of our escape."

"Do you really think so?" she questioned.

"Yes, my dear," I agreed, having perceived Holmes's brilliant deduction. "He planned everything, with the possible exception of your unannounced entrance. That is why Ling was so unpleasant with you this evening. He did so to provoke Holmes and I, in order to prompt a skirmish. He knew we would take advantage of the moment to make a go for it. Your arriving when you did only made matters easier for him."

"Very good, Watson!" Holmes chimed in with praise. "I believe you're beginning to get a feel for this work."

"Please, Holmes," I remarked, exhausted, "don't remind me."

My friend laughed briefly at my discomfort and then returned to a more reserved mood.

"Yes, Watson, I'm afraid we are to be Ling's bearers of bad tidings to Her Majesty. This surely was his plan all along."

Emily sat on the ground, dazed by the unsettling experience. Her hair was matted down by the water and her once-beautiful dress was a complete shambles. But, looking at her then, I can remember how radiant she was, even in her mussed condition.

We stood after a short rest and started walking through the woods to where we had left our horses earlier that evening.

"Emily," I spoke apologetically, "er . . . Miss Cantaville. I hope you can forgive me for calling you a Judas earlier. I mean, I . . . well, what I'm trying to say is--"

"What you are trying to say," Holmes interjected, "is that you are sorry for making a perfect ass of yourself."

"Yes," I replied, glaring peevishly at my associate for his bluntness. "I'm afraid I really put my foot in it."

"No need for apologies, Dr. Watson." The woman spoke freely, as though she had nothing to lose. "You know the worst of me now."

She continued and seemed relieved to have the truth known. "The Cantavilles are quite penniless. My poor brother, Manfred, was never one for business."

"Is what Mr. Ling said about your brother true?" I questioned. "Did he take his own life?"

"Yes, I'm afraid so," Emily answered sorrowfully. "It was kept as quiet as possible to spare me the embarrassment. I buried him about a year ago."

"Yes, I know," Holmes remarked. "That is how I knew you were concealing something when we chatted in the coach. After your brother's death, I was called in by the local authorities to rule out the possibility of foul play. You were away at that time, Watson. And, seeing how it was most evident that it was, indeed, suicide, I saw no reason to bring the matter to your attention when you returned."

"You mean," said I, "that you knew Emily was not truthful with us from the beginning?"

"Yes, my dear Watson. And after finding out that you were old acquaintances, it seemed cruel to tell you so, as I was confident you would find out soon enough. It was evident to me that Miss Cantaville could hardly have been summoned to Dover by a man who has been quite dead for almost a year."

I could see that Emily was feeling all the worse, so I sought to find some consoling factor in the matter.

"You have no other family, then?"

"No, none--except for a few distant relatives who are completely disinterested in me. I have been forced to support myself as best I can." She then became silent for a moment. I remembered Ling's remark about her virtue and struggled to make the conversation lighter.

"Well, I'm sure a woman of your charm and background is quite able to secure gainful employment."

"You need not make excuse for me, Dr. Watson. Everything Mr. Ling said is true. I made myself a woman for hire and that is that. My background, as you say, consisted of standing around

41

trying to look dignified--hardly the proper credentials for gainful employment. That is why I carry the pistols I had call to use earlier. Most of my clients are very fine gentlemen, indeed, but some tend to become a bit nasty when displaying their baser side. I'm just glad my father is not living to see it."

"What is your association with Ling?" Holmes asked. There was a distinct note of compassion in his words.

"He came to me in London and offered me a great deal of money. He said I need only ride with you to Dover and tell him everything we talked about. I assumed it was a simple matter of business and saw no harm in complying with his request. I have done some spying for other businessmen in the past, but I had no idea he was such a cruel and evil man. It would seem Mr. Ling did find himself a proper Judas."

"Don't be so hard on yourself, Miss Cantaville," Holmes said softly. "Anyone in your desperate position would have done as much. But now, Watson, I think it is time to pay Charlie a little visit. Scotland Yard needs to know of this and now's as good a time as any."

"I quite agree, Holmes."

We finally reached the horses and rose to our mounts. I stretched out my hand to Emily who seated herself behind me, her arms tight around my waist.

"May we count on your assistance, Miss Cantaville? I am sure the inspector will want to question you."

"Yes, of course, Mr. Holmes. I wish to do whatever I can to help."

We then rode off in the direction of the inn to procure another coach back to London. It was a lovely evening and the fragrance of the woods in spring filled my nostrils. I had offered Emily a ride on my mount because of our slight acquaintance, and because my associate was always one who seemed reluctant to interact with the feminine gender. But as we galloped through the night, Holmes's eyes were constantly glancing over towards us. My heart was going out to her for the sorrow and tragedy she had suffered. I had come to care for her greatly in a very short time. And, after seeing Holmes's reaction to my beautiful passenger, I began to wonder if I was alone in my feelings.

42

Chapter Three

"Ten million pounds!"

The inspector's eyes nearly popped out of his head.

"I'll have that dog clapped in irons within the week."

"Calm yourself, Charlie," was Holmes's restrained reply. "You'll do nothing of the sort. Any attempt to incarcerate Mr. Ling at this time would only result in disaster for the city."

Charlie slammed his fist on the table, knocking over his tea.

"Blast it, Holmes, can he really do such a thing?"

"He most certainly can, Inspector," I interjected. "Make no mistake about that."

Charlie sank slowly back in his chair. "I must tell you, gentlemen, if anyone else but yourselves had come to me with such a story, I would have laughed them to scorn."

"I know, Charlie," Holmes spoke softly, "that is why Ling chose us. I'm sure of it."

It was then that the good inspector glanced at our lovely companion seated in a chair near the doorway of the briefing room where we were.

"Is this the woman you told me about?"

"Ah . . . yes, Inspector," I said, stumbling over my words, "the one who came to our assistance."

Charlie rose and moved towards her, changing his scowl to a pleasant smile in an instant.

"How wonderful to make your acquaintance, my dear. Mr. Holmes and Dr. Watson have told me of your great courage."

Holmes and I had, indeed, told Charlie everything, although we were careful to omit the portion about Emily's destitute condition and questionable profession.

"How did the analysis of the gunpowder turn out?" I asked, already knowing the answer.

"Not so well, I'm afraid." The inspector smiled at Emily once more, and then rejoined us at the table.

43

"We were unable to determine the complete composition of the substance. After several attempts failed, we decided to take what was left of the powder and detonate it."

Holmes's eyebrows raised in concern.

"What were the results, Inspector?"

"Well," Charlie remarked, a bit embarrassed, "Sergeant Riggs was temporarily flash-blinded by the experiment, but he regained his sight after a few hours. Fortunately he was far enough away from the blast that he was not injured."

The inspector railed on us now. "What in heaven's name is it, gentlemen! There wasn't enough powder left to fill a thimble, and yet it nearly took the roof off our explosives room. If Sergeant Riggs were not such an experienced man, I could have lost him."

"I warned you, Charlie," Holmes insisted. "The substance is several times more volatile than anything we know of."

The inspector seated himself at the briefing table and took on the air of a more calm individual. Charlie was, indeed, a professional, although he was given to an occasional lack of vision. But his instincts told him it was now time for clear thinking.

"All right, gentlemen, I suppose the first thing to be done is to notify the Prime Minister and Her Majesty."

"I took the liberty of speaking with Benjamin Disraeli before we came to you, Inspector."

"Well, Holmes," Charlie sighed, looking genuinely sad, "I suppose you did the right thing. By now he has spoken to the Queen, and our grand lady will have another sleepless night to look forward to."

I looked at Charlie, not knowing what to say. Just then the inspector's secretary approached us and handed him a note.

"Gentlemen, Her Majesty and the Prime Minister have requested a meeting with us in one hour. Do you have any of the powder left, Holmes?"

"I'm sorry, Inspector, I gave you all of it. We'll have to present our case with the simple power of persuasion."

"It's not the Queen and the Prime Minister I'm worried about," Charlie remarked. "It's Parliament that concerns me. I question whether or not they will take such a threat seriously."

Emily had remained silent all through our conversation, but now she stood from her chair and addressed us.

"If you gentlemen will excuse me, I will take my leave of you now. There is really nothing I can add to what Mr. Holmes and Dr. Watson have already told you, Inspector Whittington. I will leave my address with your secretary and you may feel free to contact me at any time."

"Yes, of course, my dear." Charlie approached her with true compassion. "You have been through a terrible ordeal and I'm sure you require some rest."

The inspector drew close to her and almost whispered, "You will, of course, say nothing of this matter to anyone, not even your most intimate acquaintances? If word of this were to get out, you understand, it could cause a panic among the general population."

"Yes, Inspector, I understand completely. You have my full assurance of silence and my total cooperation."

"Thank you, my dear. I will be calling on you soon."

With that, Emily walked over to the inspector's secretary and hurriedly scratched her address on a slip of paper. As she was leaving I met her near the exit and sought, as best I could, to alleviate her fears.

"Please don't be afraid, Emily. Everything will be all right." I choked with the words. "May I see you out?"

She looked at me with soft eyes and smiled halfheartedly. "Thank you, Dr. Watson . . . John. But that really won't be necessary. I'm perfectly fine. Good night to you all then, gentlemen."

I found it hard to let her leave so abruptly after all that we'd been through together.

"Please, Emily, let me at least hail you a cab."

"All right then, John."

I turned sheepishly to Holmes and the inspector.

"I'll only be a few moments, gentlemen."

"Take your time, Watson," Holmes said, seemingly uninterested. "Charlie and I will finish things here."

My associate appeared to be his usual complacent self. But as we turned to go, I caught the slightest hint of something different in Holmes's eyes.

Emily and I then left the room and made our way down the stairs to the street in front of Scotland Yard. Looking in both directions, I was secretly pleased to see that the thoroughfare was rather empty that evening.

"Well, not to worry, my dear, I'm sure something will be along directly."

We strolled down to the corner and found a bench to rest ourselves on while we waited.

"I suppose you're looking forward to another coach ride, considering how pleasant our passage was from Dover last night."

I was joking, of course. The trip to London had been as rough as ever, and had made it nearly impossible for us to get any sleep.

"Oh, I really don't mind, John. I was never one who required much rest. A few hours in bed and I'll be right again."

Emily suddenly blushed as we both recalled her embarrassing means of support.

"Please, Dr. Watson," she became most uncomfortable, "you needn't wait with me. I'm well able to manage for myself."

"Emily," I spoke boldly now, "I don't care who you are, or what you do for your living. I have come to care for you deeply and nothing else matters to me."

"Oh, dear!" was her surprised answer. "I had no idea, John."

"Didn't you?" I asked, moving towards her.

Just then a cab came into sight and I stood reluctantly to signal the driver. He pulled alongside us and bade us good evening.

"Oh, dear," Emily repeated, "I don't know what to say."

"Then don't say anything."

With that, I leaned forward and kissed her.

"May I call on you tomorrow?"

"Well . . . yes, I would be honored," she replied.

She then stepped quickly into the coach, and I watched as the hansom disappeared into the foggy night.

I stood there motionless for the longest time, just taking in the moment.

"Are you about, Watson!"

It was Holmes calling to me from the Yard's front gate.

"Yes, here. Are we ready to leave for the palace?"

"Yes, Watson, the driver should be here soon."

I walked back to where Holmes and Charlie were standing and tried to clear my head.

"Well, Watson," Charlie remarked, "I've ordered security doubled at the museum. Holmes pointed out to me that the Ming treasures were of great interest to Mr. Ling. He may not move against the city until he's made at least one attempt to procure them."

"Yes, I quite agree," I answered, still a bit off-balance from my encounter with Emily. "A brilliant deduction, Holmes."

"Thank you, Watson, but I'm sure you would have figured it out yourself eventually."

"Whatever you say, Holmes."

It was obvious to my associate that I was not myself, so he let it alone. Shortly after, our coach arrived and we began making our way towards the palace.

The inspector made light conversation at first, but then got to what was really on his mind.

"Miss Cantaville is a very pleasant woman indeed, but you realize that I will have to know the details about her soon enough."

I suddenly came to the realization that Charlie was not the most prominent inspector at Scotland Yard for nothing. He had, of course, realized that we were not complete in our account of the previous evening, when it came to explaining the reasons for Emily's presence in the matter.

Holmes jumped in quickly.

"It was necessary to omit certain information about Miss Cantaville, Charlie, in order to avoid undue embarrassment for her. I'll fill in the gaps for you later."

My friend glanced at me briefly, letting the inspector know that it would be better if I were not around when he did so.

"I thought nothing to the contrary, gentlemen," Charlie remarked, and then dropped the subject.

We continued our trip in silence for a short while, but then the inspector posed an interesting question.

"How much time do we have then--that is, to comply with Ling's demands?"

"We're not really sure, Charlie," Holmes answered. "Miss Cantaville intervened before he was able to make it known to us. Not to worry, though; there's little doubt that that bit of information will be forthcoming."

We finally reached the gates of the palace and were promptly received by the Prime Minister, Benjamin Disraeli. He greeted us warmly, as was his typical manner, but I could see that time was taking its toll on my old friend.

A man in his mid-seventies, Disraeli stood tall and thin, his long coat tails making him seem all the more lanky. He was gray, wrinkled, and worn from his many years of service to queen and country as statesman and prime minister. He showed his deterioration plainly, and with good reason.

Disraeli's party was swiftly losing support in Parliament, and it would be only a matter of time before he was ousted by Gladstone, his greatest rival and the man who would later replace him as prime minister. But despite his political troubles and the crisis he now faced, his mood was relatively cheerful.

Although he was several years my senior, we enjoyed a warm relationship, as he had been a friend of my family for many years. I chatted with him happily about the old days as he led us to a large sitting-room on the third floor where the meeting was to take place.

"Make yourselves comfortable, gentlemen." Disraeli spoke now with a more reserved tone. "Her Majesty will be with us shortly."

"How is our grand lady?" Charlie inquired with a note of apprehension in his voice. "Was it hard for her?"

I could see the old statesman's eyes become dim.

"Yes, Inspector Whittington, the news was a blow to her. But unless you know her as I have come to know her, it would not be evident to you."

Just then, the large double doors of the sitting-room opened and our beloved Victoria entered. Dressed more commonly than one might expect, she had obviously been in her bed by the time Disraeli had reached her with the frightful news. But although her dress was plain, the woman's presence dominated the room, leaving no doubt that this was, indeed, a Queen.

"You will forgive me, gentlemen, if I remain casual. It is late--much too late for proper protocol."

"Of course, Your Majesty," we said, almost in unison, as Disraeli escorted our grand lady to a small circle of chairs which had been arranged in such a way that we could see the queen and a breathtaking view of the city through a large window behind where she was seated.

"Thank you, Dizzy," she remarked as we settled into the chairs around her.

"Dizzy" was the queen's pet name for Disraeli, as he was her most trusted counselor. She was always quite affectionate towards him, and since the death of her husband Prince Albert he was always at her side in time of crisis.

"Let us not belabor the matter, gentlemen. There seems to be a madman about who is demanding the lifeblood of England."

She looked directly at Holmes.

"Tell me, sir, is there any reason why I should take this man seriously?"

"There is indeed, Your Majesty. He has the power to destroy all of London in one swift stroke. Everything the Prime Minister has told you is true. We have no defense against such a weapon."

"Can you tell me then," she continued, "should this be considered an act of war from the nation of China?"

"No, Your Majesty," Holmes was quick to answer. "I do not believe so. This Ling fellow seems to be acting on his own behalf. I do not think the Chinese government is aware of his actions."

She paused for a moment in thought. "Should we then consider calling in the Chinese authorities?"

"Not at this time," my friend replied.

"Yes, I quite agree," Charlie interjected.

Holmes continued, "We are the ones who have the most to lose at this time. I think it would be best if we resolve this matter ourselves."

"And how do you suggest we resolve the matter, Mr. Holmes?"

"Your Majesty," Charlie interrupted, "I feel strongly that no ransom should be paid; at least, not yet."

"Do you, Inspector? Would you agree, Mr. Holmes?"

"Yes, Your Majesty, I would."

Charlie looked at my associate, a bit bewildered. I believe he had fully expected him to disagree.

Holmes spoke again. "I am convinced that Ling means to destroy London whether he is paid his ransom or not. I believe he intends to make an example of us to China and the rest of the world."

The queen sat motionless for a moment contemplating Holmes's morbid conjecture. She then rose, still silent, and walked to the open window overlooking the city.

"If this is so, then it would seem that we are doomed, gentlemen."

Holmes sprang to his feet. "It need not be so, Your Majesty!"

"Indeed, Mr. Holmes. You yourself have said that we have no defense against such a weapon."

"Yes, I did say so," my friend said as he moved towards her, "but that does not mean that this man cannot be stopped. It is true that his power is formidable, and we must take the greatest caution in dealing with him, but I am convinced that he can be overcome."

The queen gazed at my companion now with hopeful eyes. She seemed moved by his words and her expression revealed her curiosity with him.

"I have heard of your cleverness, sir. Solver of riddles, puzzle master, finder of secrets--all these have I heard you called. Inspector Whittington has told me that you know what a man will do even before he himself knows."

Holmes stood speechless for a moment. He seemed to almost blush. "Well, Your Majesty, sometimes these stories of me are a bit exaggerated."

With that, the queen reached into the pocket of her dress and proclaimed, "Can anyone in this room tell me what I have in my pocket?"

We all looked at each other, wide-eyed in astonishment. All, that is, except Holmes, who seemed quite ready to answer.

"What do I have in my pocket, Dizzy?" she demanded.

The prime minister smiled, but then humored the queen's strange request by venturing a guess.

"Perhaps it is my lady's comb."

"Not so, Dizzy," she replied politely. "Inspector?"

Charlie stammered a bit and then answered. "I'm not sure, Your Majesty."

"Come, come, Inspector," she prompted, "you must make a guess."

Charlie was quite obviously uncomfortable, but did as she asked. "Could it be a key to something?"

"No, it could not," she answered, and then turned her attentions to me. "Dr. Watson?"

I had spent the time listening to the others reply and was startled that my turn had come so quickly.

"Is it, perhaps, a jewel of some sort?"

"No, Doctor, but that is a pleasant thought."

She then looked to my associate, who had remained quite patient as we answered. "Can you tell me what I have in my pocket, Mr. Holmes?"

We waited with great apprehension to see if he could, indeed, solve this seemingly unsolvable riddle.

"Yes, Your Majesty. You have your hand in your pocket."

At that, a broad smile slowly formed on her tired face.

"Why, of course she has her hand in her pocket," Charlie protested. "Anyone could see that."

"Then why did you not tell me so, Inspector?" she replied.

"Well, I . . ."

She did not wait for him to answer. Instead, she approached Holmes and took his hand. "Then you will see to it that this Ling fellow does not destroy all that we have."

"Yes, Queen Mother, you have my word as an Englishman."

"And I shall expect you to keep it." She winked at Holmes and then looked to Disraeli.

"Dizzy, it will be our work to convince Parliament that the matter is to be left to Scotland Yard and these gentlemen. Inspector Whittington, the entire military and whatever funds and materials you require will be placed at your disposal."

She looked Charlie square in the eyes. "In a sense, Inspector, I am granting you unlimited authority, until such time as this crisis is resolved. The Prime Minister will see to it that you are given everything you require."

The queen then looked at Holmes almost apologetically. It was evident that she had no choice but to put Charlie in charge of things. He was, after all, the government official in this matter and she could hardly choose a civilian over him, despite my associate's obvious qualifications.

"Mr. Holmes and Dr. Watson, I shall expect you to give Inspector Whittington your complete support. And, Inspector, I shall expect you to use it."

"Of course, Your Majesty," Charlie replied. "I shall not fail you, my Queen."

Holmes had nodded his approval to the queen's decision, but although it was not readily evident, I could tell that he was troubled within.

Charlie was, indeed, a capable man, of that there was no doubt. But the inspector tended to rely more on his feelings, sometimes, than the facts. And while instinct is a crucial quality in a good detective, Charlie had a bad habit of acting before things were completely thought out.

Nevertheless, Holmes extended his hand to the inspector. "We're with you, Charlie."

"Thank you, Holmes," he answered. "I'm sure we'll do well together."

I, too, gave Charlie my hand, but I was secretly as uneasy as my associate.

"Your Majesty," Holmes remarked, "I think it would be best if you left for Balmoral as soon as possible."

Balmoral, in Scotland, is of course, the queen's summer residence, and we were all anxious to see her leave, considering the danger that everyone within London was exposed to.

"I shall not be leaving just yet. There is much work to be done here."

"Your Majesty," Disraeli protested, "you know that I am well able to handle matters here. Mr. Holmes is right. The sooner you leave London, the better."

We all chimed in and prevailed upon our queen to flee the city as soon as possible. But her mind was set and nothing could move her--not even Ling's dragons.

"I shall remain in London so long as she is in peril. If the worst should come . . ." she paused now, as though the words were too terrible to be spoken, "if the worst should come, I will be with my people. It is a Queen's right to die with her people."

We were left speechless. It was evident that she would do as she willed, and that nothing we said could move her to change her decision. She stepped once more to the large window overlooking the city and gazed out over the distant rooftops.

It was a lovely sight, indeed, as the soft light from the street lamps gave a dreamlike appearance to the familiar old buildings below.

"I will say good evening to you now, gentlemen," she said, still staring at the spectacle. "The best to you all, and God go with you."

"Good evening, Your Majesty." We spoke again, as one, as we moved towards the exit.

"Mr. Holmes," the queen called as we neared the doorway, "will you please come here for a moment?"

My associate walked over to her. To our surprise, she whispered something to him. Holmes smiled and kissed her hand.

"Thank you, my lady. I am deeply grateful."

With that, he rejoined us and we returned to the courtyard where our coach was still waiting. Holmes and I boarded, but

Charlie remained behind with Disraeli to discuss his new authority.

"Good evening, gentlemen," Charlie said as we prepared to go. "Let's meet in my office first thing in the morning and plan our strategy."

"Yes, of course. Eight o'clock sharp," Holmes answered.

I remember the most uneasy feeling I had as we said our good-byes to the inspector and the prime minister. It disturbed me greatly, as I surmised that I was reacting to my friend, who had suddenly become quite morbid. Holmes had said a swift good-bye and quickly hidden himself within the coach.

We then sped off into the night towards Baker Street.

Holmes was a man given to many moods, and sometimes very gloomy ones at that. But I had never seen him so somber as he was that night.

I thought to lighten his spirit a bit, and ventured a little joke, in the hope of bringing him out of it.

"So, now you have secrets with the Queen. Tell me, have you been taking tea with Her Majesty behind my back?"

"He will make the error, Watson."

"What did you say, Holmes?"

My friend was staring without expression into the quiet London evening. "He will make the fatal error."

"Who? Charlie! Come now, Holmes, I know that Charlie can be a bit impetuous at times but--"

"You know it yourself, Watson." He now looked at me with knowing eyes. "I've been with you long enough to have discovered it. You keep the manner of a simple physician, but your face reveals your understanding."

I was shocked beyond words. It was as though my mind were glass and he could see my every thought. For in my quiet way, I believed that I had fooled him all this time. But he seemed to know me better than I knew myself.

"Yes, Holmes, you're . . . you're right, of course. Charlie will make the fatal error."

The words were heavy on my lips. For although I, too, had realized it in the back of my mind, I could not bring myself to admit the worst. All my hope had suddenly vanished, and I gave way to despair.

"We must find some way to get Her Majesty and as many of the population as possible out of London before it is too late. There is nothing else to be done."

My companion turned again to look at me with wide eyes, as his somber expression suddenly left him with remarkable speed.

"My dear Watson, please forgive me."

"What do you mean, Holmes?"

"I had forgotten how sensitive you really are. I'm such a moody chap. I didn't realize what I was doing to you. My occasional flights of fancy are simply my way of deducing certain problems. I must imagine myself in the most precarious of situations in order to reason out the proper solutions. But you really didn't understand that, did you? My poor Watson--too much worry and too little sleep. Yes, my friend, Charlie will make the fatal error. And we shall be there to stop him.

"Once we reach home, you shall have a good night's rest. And should Charlie, or anyone else, come to disturb us this evening, I will prevent them from waking you--of that you may rest assured."

Again I was speechless. "Well, ah . . . thank you, old man."

Holmes then smiled a broad, cheerful smile. And, although he was one rarely given to signs of affection, he reached out and patted me reassuringly on the shoulder.

"My good Watson. What a gift from God you really are."

Now encouraged by my associate's new enthusiasm, I ventured another question.

"Where are we to begin then, Holmes?"

"I haven't the slightest idea, Watson," he said, still smiling. "But not to worry, something will come along."

I smiled halfheartedly back to him, for it was not exactly the answer I had hoped to hear.

The coach now arrived at our apartment, and as we stepped out Holmes threw a coin to the driver. This, of course, antagonized him, for he was a Scotland Yard regular. It was my associate's way of having a little laugh, and he chuckled to himself all the way up the steps to the door. I chuckled a bit myself, but scolded him for his rude joke.

"Why do you give those poor fellows such a bad time of it?"

"Because, my dear Watson, it helps to keep their noses a bit more level with the ground."

As I put my key in the door, Holmes noticed a small envelope tucked in the hinge.

"What have we here?"

My associate opened it and read aloud:

"This night the moon shines full, then sets upon the mire. When hence the moon is full again, then comes the dragon's fire."

He paused for a moment in thought. "Well, Watson, now we know when."

"What do you mean, when?"

"If Ming's demands are not met by the next full moon, he will launch his rockets on London."

"You mean Ling, don't you, Holmes?"

"What did you say, Watson?"

"You called him Ming, but you meant Ling."

"Oh, yes, of course. But no matter. Willy is here and perhaps he has found something for us."

Willy was Holmes's informant in the city. He kept mostly to the back streets and was my associate's eyes and ears in the less desirable parts of London. He was a sullen, rat-faced little man, who always crept into our apartment while we were out and waited in the shadows for our return.

"How do you always know when Willy is here?" I asked, as I opened the door.

"Use your nose, Watson. Don't you smell it?"

I sniffed the air for a moment, but could detect nothing out of the ordinary.

"I'm sorry, old man, but I don't know what you mean."

"Try again, Watson," Holmes prompted.

And so I did. Presently, the most fragile fragrance of stale perfume became evident to me. Willy had a weakness for the ladies, and probably used the money Holmes paid to him to frequent the shady houses and bordellos that were plentiful in Willy's territory.

"Oh, yes," I remarked, a bit amazed by my friend's keen senses.

We went directly into the study, as that was always where he hid himself.

"You can show yourself now, Willy," Holmes said as he hung his coat on the rack.

Two timid, mouselike eyes peered out from a dark corner of the room.

"Good evenin', gov'nors."

"Good evening, Willy," I echoed. "You can come out."

The shy little man moved quickly to a high-backed chair near the desk, but was careful to keep from view of the large window.

"What do you have for us tonight, then?" Holmes inquired, seating himself on the sofa directly across from him.

"Someone's lookin' for you, Mr. 'olmes. Says 'e wants to 'ave a meetin'."

"Indeed, and who might this someone be?"

"Don't know 'is proper name. But I do know 'e's a Chinaman. And I 'ear tell 'e calls 'imself Guardian."

"Guardian, you say?"

"That's right, Mr. 'olmes. Been askin' for you all over. Don't know what it is 'e wants, but I do know 'e's lookin'."

"I see. Is there anything else you can tell me, Willy?"

"That's all I know, sir, except . . ." he paused as though afraid to speak.

"Except what?" Holmes prodded.

"Well, sir, I'm told 'e 'as two other Chinamen with 'im and I 'ear tell they're bloody dangerous."

"What do you mean, dangerous?"

"I 'eared from a friend that they were jumped in an alley by Tommy Pritchert and 'is boys, and they left old Tom with two arms broken."

This was quite a surprise. Tom Pritchert and his band of thugs were notorious in London for petty theft and assault. They always traveled in numbers so as to overcome their victims with force. But this time it appeared they had stumbled into a small hornet's nest.

"Well, Mr. Holmes," I chuckled, "it couldn't have happened to a nicer fellow."

"Right you are, Watson," he replied, laughing. "Anything else then, Willy?"

"No, sir, that's all I 'ave."

"All right then." Holmes stood and placed a few notes of currency on the desk.

"Keep your eyes and ears open, Willy. And let me know as soon as you have anything else."

"Right you are, Mr. 'olmes."

The odd little man rose quickly and snatched the notes from the desk, tucking them into his shirt. "Pleasant evenin', gov'nors."

With that, he all but ran to a small window that was located on the side of the room farthest away from the street lamps, and was gone in an instant.

"What do you make of it, Holmes? Some of Ling's people?"

"I'm not sure, Watson. It could possibly be. Oh, well, not much more we can do tonight. Let's get some sleep. We'll be knocking up early to meet with Charlie in the morning."

"Right you are," I agreed. "Sleep is just the thing."

We retired to our bedrooms and, I dare say, I was out sound the moment my head touched the pillow. But as exhausted as I was, my mind still registered the noise which emanated from the sitting-room downstairs. The clock showed that only a few hours had passed, so I dismissed it as a dream. But after closing my eyes for a few moments, I heard it once more."

"Watson," Holmes whispered outside my door.

"Yes, Holmes, I hear it," was my soft reply.

"Do you have a pistol?"

"Yes," I answered.

Having lost Mildred to Mr. Ling, I had procured another from Scotland Yard, but it was one of the Yard's standard issue and the weapon felt awkward in my hand. How I missed my Mildred as we made our way cautiously down the stairs in our night clothes.

"They're in the study now, Watson. You go right and I'll go left."

"Yes, as usual, Holmes."

Whenever we entered a room that might hold peril, we always split to give each other cover in the event of a shooting match.

I could see the room was dimly lit by a single lamp, as we moved silently down the narrow hall which led to the study. My associate and I took a deep breath and then rushed into the room--rolling on the floor and coming to rest with our pistols trained on two intruders.

They were both Chinese. One of the men was holding a small lantern, and it was evident from the look on their faces that we had taken them by complete surprise.

"Who are you, and what do you want?" demanded Holmes.

With wide and startled eyes, one of the men blurted, "God save the Queen."

Holmes and I were stunned by his statement.

"What did you say, old man?" I asked, quite puzzled.

He repeated the phrase as though it were a question.

"God save the Queen?"

"What do you think, Holmes?" said I.

With that, the Oriental barked, "Holmes! Letter for Holmes!"

He reached into his shirt as though searching for something. A moment later he produced a small white envelope and held it out in the direction of my companion. "Letter for Holmes."

"Keep an eye on them, Watson, and I'll take a look."

"Right you are, Holmes."

My associate took great care in approaching the curious strangers, but soon had the envelope in hand. He opened it and digested the information quickly.

"It appears to be from that Guardian fellow Willy told us about. He says that these two chaps are his sons and that they do not speak English. I suppose he taught them a few phrases against the advent of our meeting like this."

Holmes looked at me with regret.

"It goes on to say that if we go along with these two fellows, they will bring us to meet with someone in order that we might discuss the dilemma of the three dragons. What do you think, Watson? Can you go on, with what little sleep you've had?"

I moaned a bit as I thought of my warm bed, but I knew my associate would be going--with or without me.

"Why not? It seems to be in keeping with everything else that's happened so far. You know, Holmes, it could be a trap."

"Yes, that is a definite possibility, Watson."

"Let's get changed," I said, realizing as well as my friend that, considering the absence of any other leads, it was a chance that had to be taken.

After a brief search of their persons, we locked our two visitors in my bedroom closet while we changed. I could hear them chattering to one another as I dressed and couldn't help but wonder what they might lead us to. Soon after, Holmes came in and we released the men from their tiny prison.

"All right then, gentlemen," said Holmes, "let's get started."

We left my bedroom and proceeded towards the stairway at the end of the hall. My associate and I began to descend, but the Orientals beckoned us to stop with their arms waving. Pointing at the ceiling, they began walking upstairs towards the upper rooms that were inhabited by Mrs. Hudson and a few of the other tenants.

"Where are they going, Holmes?" I asked.

"Well, Watson, if I were to venture a guess, I would have to say the roof."

"The roof?" I could make no sense of it.

We followed them up the stairs and down the narrow hallway of the third floor. Sure enough, they brought us directly to the ladder which led up to the rooftop.

Sending the two Orientals on first, Holmes quickly followed, but paused as he poked his head through the small opening above us. Having stopped dead in his tracks, he looked back down at me with a most unusual expression.

"Why don't you let me take care of this one, Watson? You haven't had nearly enough sleep. I'll give you a full report in the morning."

"Don't be ridiculous, Holmes," I replied, quite bewildered. "I'm going with you, of course. Now finish your climb so I can get off this ladder."

Shrugging his shoulders, he stepped onto the roof and extended his arm to give me a hand up. I had been on the roof before and was looking forward to the beautiful view I remembered. But as I stepped up, I could see that the sight was blocked by a large object only a few feet away. It took a moment for my eyes to adjust to the darkness, but slowly the unbelievable thing came into focus.

"It's a boat!" I exclaimed, not knowing what to think.

About twenty feet in length, it rested on its keel while several wires, or cables, extended up from both sides. These were attached to a long, cigar-shaped object which hovered above the ship. Upon closer examination, it became evident to me that the object above the boat was some sort of balloon which was decorated with a multitude of Chinese symbols and markings.

"What in heaven's name is that?" I asked, absolutely stunned.

"I believe, Watson," said Holmes, very matter-of-factly, "that this is our transportation for the evening."

I, quite frankly, nearly dropped my teeth. For it was evident by the way the two Orientals were preparing the craft that it was, indeed, some sort of sky vessel being made ready for launching.

"Oh, no," I blurted in protest, "not in that monstrosity!"

"I'm sure I can handle this one, Watson. Go back to bed."

"I will indeed," was my adamant reply. "A man would have to be missing most of his faculties to ride in such a thing--not to mention in the dark as well."

"Yes, Watson, I'm sure they took advantage of the cover of night. Very clever, indeed. It would have been nearly impossible for anyone to have followed. What navigators they must be, to have found us in the darkness."

Just then the two men leapt into the odd-looking craft and waved at us to board.

"Stay and get your rest, Watson. I'll return as soon as possible."

My friend stepped in and motioned his readiness to the men. They began to cast off, releasing their lines, which caused the sky ship to rise slowly.

"Blast it, Holmes, who'll guard your back! You're outnumbered two to one as it is."

I hurried forward and caught the edge of the ship's railing. As the ship continued upward, it carried me, dangling, out over the city.

"Pull me up, Holmes! Do you hear!"

"Watson," he said, looking over the side with a snide smile, "I'm sure the view is quite wonderful from there, but won't you join us?"

"Quite funny, Holmes," I said angrily. "Now pull me up!"

My associate reached over the side and grabbed me by my belt from behind. With one mighty yank he had me on board, sprawled face down on the deck. Looking up, I could see one of the Orientals smiling at me from his place in the front of the ship. I smiled back at him as Holmes helped me onto the bench.

"The first one of them that looks at us sideways," I remarked, still smiling, "is going to get his ears shot off."

The men had positioned themselves, one to the front, and the other to the extreme rear of the vessel. Holmes and I were about midway. The man behind was operating a strange mechanism, which was delivering a blast of air from a valve he controlled. This, I guessed, was our means of propulsion. A very clever device--it was set on a pivot so that he could also control our direction with it, like a rudder. The man in front of us held a line in his hand which extended up to what looked like another small valve directly under the balloon. All of this appeared to be attached to a central engine of some kind, located under the deck beneath us.

"I'll watch the one in front, Holmes, and you keep an eye on that fellow back there."

"Relax a bit, Watson. I think if they were going to try something, they'd have done so by now."

It was then that the fellow in front of us pulled on his line. We heard a hissing sound and suddenly perceived that we were rising ever faster.

"Fascinating," Holmes opined.

"Well, I suppose so," I replied, "but I have seen hot air balloons before."

"That's just it, Watson. It's not hot air. It appears to be some type of gas that is unusually buoyant in the atmosphere. I've never seen anything like it."

I remembered reading something about the theories of lighter-than-air gases, but was too occupied with our flight to mention it to Holmes.

We had raised well above the lights of the city now, and were traveling in a northeasterly direction.

The view of our quiet London was breathtaking. I could see the whole of the city from this altitude and the rooftops of all the buildings. The palace was in plain sight, as was the Tower of London. It all unnerved me greatly because I was never one fond of heights. But there was something else that was nagging at me. A feeling. A feeling that I had seen this picture before. But where?

It suddenly came to me like a shot. It was the view I had observed while studying Ling's scale replica of our fair city, sprawled across the large table in Morlock Castle. I also perceived that it was the sight that Ling's frightful dragons would see an instant before they rained their terrible destruction down upon the innocent people sleeping so unaware in their beds below.

We moved along gracefully on the wind. In fact, the ride was so quiet and peaceful that I found myself nodding off now and then.

Once over the countryside, the earth became dark and we could see the lights of the city fading in the distance behind us. Suddenly, the man in front pulled on another line. We heard the hissing sound again and could feel the skyship begin to descend.

"Where are they bringing us, Holmes? I can't see a thing below."

"There, Watson."

Turning in the direction my associate had indicated, I spied a single, tiny dot of light shining through the black expanse beneath us.

"These men are most remarkable navigators, indeed," Holmes observed.

Our descent was rapid now, and we could begin to distinguish the shape of a rather large structure in the moonlight.

"Another castle!" I exclaimed. "Why is it that all our old castles are now being inhabited by the Chinese?"

"It's the Wellingshire Castle, Watson. Can you see the shape of the towers?"

I nodded to my companion in agreement as we settled onto our landing point. The Oriental behind us leapt onto the roof and secured a line, while his friend was quick to join him. In a matter of moments we docked, and they motioned to us to follow them once more."

"I don't like it, Holmes. There's no telling how many could be waiting inside."

"I know, my friend. But, again, we have very little choice."

We followed the two peculiar men--who were still smiling at us and chattering incessantly--through the doorway of one of the large towers. Inside we found a spiral staircase that coiled downward into the bowels of the old structure.

Wellingshire Castle, like Morlock Castle, had sat empty for many years. It was still owned by the Wellingshire family, but while the outer appearance of the building and the grounds were well kept, the interior of the castle had been forsaken. It was well-known that the Wellingshire family retained it mainly as a historic curiosity, and also as a matter of family pride.

We continued our trek downward, taking care to look for anything out of the ordinary. Once on the ground floor, our guides led us to the old dining hall located near the center of the building. It was a spacious room with a high ceiling supported by several marble pillars. But it had been completely stripped of all furnishings except for a large, Oriental rug that lay on the floor in the middle of the decaying room.

"What now, gentlemen?" I asked as the men paused in this place.

They spoke to us in Chinese, pointing to the rug on the floor, and then began to leave. Holmes and I started to follow again, but one of the men motioned us back with a hand gesture.

"I believe they wish us to remain here, Watson."

With that, the two young men left the hall and closed the large double doors of the entryway.

"Take hold of a torch, Watson, and let's inspect a bit."

I pulled one down, as did my associate, and began checking the floors and walls.

"I suppose you get tired of my asking, Holmes, but what exactly is it we're looking for?"

As I spoke, I began to cross the room over the Oriental rug.

"I'm not sure, Watson. But I think we'll know when we find it."

An instant later, I reached the center of the room and suddenly felt my feet lose the floor. A moment after that, I found myself sitting in darkness with an excruciating pain shooting up my spine.

I had fallen through a concealed opening in the floor and landed square on my rump in some sort of lower chamber located underneath the dining hall. Holmes, fearing what had become of me, appeared swiftly at the edge and looked in to see if I was all together. He was quick to observe that I was generally all right and, being rather mischievous by nature, could not resist prodding my ego a bit.

"What are you doing down there, Watson?"

"I'm knitting a sweater, Holmes," was my sarcastic reply.

"Are you indeed?" He chuckled. "Well, let me bring you a light so you won't strain your eyes."

My companion joined me presently and helped me to my feet.

"Oh, my back," I complained as I stood. "I tell you, Holmes, sometimes I rue the day we said hello."

"Do you." He laughed as he relit my torch. "Next time try the stairs, Watson, then you won't have this problem."

"Stairs, indeed," I grumbled as we peered about trying to establish where we were.

"There's a passageway in this direction," Holmes observed. "It seems to be the one and only."

"Then I suppose that's the way we should go," I grumbled.

Torches in hand, we set off down the narrow tunnel. I had had my fill of it by now, and drew my regulation pistol to satisfy my apprehension.

"Musty old place," I continued my complaint. "Reminds me of the Paris sewers, which I did not care for either, I might add."

I suppose Holmes had grown accustomed to my occasional bad temper, as he walked on seemingly unaffected by my foul mood.

"And this pistol is as clumsy as a brick. How I wish I had Mildred."

We continued on for a long space, winding around in several directions, when finally we entered a dark room. It felt wonderful to be out of close quarters again.

"There are torches on the walls, Watson. Let's light a few and see what's about."

We did just that. But to my surprise, the illumination revealed that we had stumbled into the castle's ancient torture chamber. An iron maiden hung from the ceiling, while a rack was setting near one wall. The room was filled with all sorts of decaying contraptions whose sole purpose had been the agonizing destruction of the human person. It was for me a painful reminder of our barbaric past.

"Well, now I've seen it all, Holmes. What a repulsive sight."

"Not very pretty, is it, my friend?"

Just then a loud creaking sound caused us to spin around. An old wooden door on the far side of the room was opening slowly. I leveled my weapon on the spot.

"Good evening, gentlemen," a soft voice spoke. "There is no need to defend yourself, Dr. Watson. You are in no danger."

It was hard to see in the flickering light of the torches, so I called a warning.

"Identify yourself, sir!"

"Of course," was the shadow's reply. "I am the Guardian."

He pushed the door wide open now, and we could see the form of an elderly Chinese gentleman who was dressed in traditional Far Eastern garments. He was a short fellow with white hair and beard. At first glance he reminded me a bit of an Oriental Father Christmas.

"Please come in and accept my hospitality, gentlemen. You will find it much more pleasant in here."

I was still reluctant, but Holmes followed the little man, as did I, my pistol still in hand.

As we entered the room, I could see that it had been decorated and furnished quite completely, causing a sharp contrast to my senses from the dreary chamber we had just left.

"I hope you will forgive the inconvenience which you experienced in the dining hall earlier," the old man said while lighting a small pipe. "I realized the instant it happened that my sons had failed to caution you properly."

"How did you know we had stumbled into your trap, sir?" I asked.

"It has been necessary for me to take certain . . . precautions while in your country. There are those here that I am seeking who do not wish to be found."

"Tell me, Mr. Guardian," Holmes inquired, "just who is it that you seek?"

"Ah, yes, Mr. Holmes, that does bring us to the heart of the matter."

The small chap seated himself comfortably and bid us to do the same. It was then that the two young Orientals who had brought us to this place entered through a small door on the far side of the room.

"Let me begin by introducing my two sons. The eldest is Soong and the younger is Wu--my last born. In all, I have five sons and two daughters, but only these children are with me."

I carefully reexamined the scrapping young men he called children, who smiled and bowed in acknowledgement when he mentioned their names.

"My name is Lee Ho. You know me as Guardian, as do many of the people in my country. But my true family name is Ming."

Now Holmes's eyes brightened, as he seemed to be piecing the puzzle together quickly.

"Tell me, Mr. Ming, why are you called Guardian?" Holmes spoke excitedly, as though his answer would finish the riddle.

"In the year 1644--this according to your calendar--the Ming rulers of China faced invasion and defeat by the Manchus warriors from the north. Many great and wonderful secrets had been discovered in China during the period you know as the Ming dynasty; secrets about the ways of nature and the special materials that can be obtained from the earth. Because it was necessary to keep these secrets from the enemy, my ancestors--members of the Emperor's family--were commanded to take the books of knowledge and flee to the South. Although most of the royal family was executed, my ancestors survived by roaming from village to village, and by changing the family name to Ling."

"Excuse me, sir," I interrupted, "but did you say Ling?"

"Yes, Dr. Watson. I believe you are beginning to understand. For over two hundred years we have been known as the guardians of the books. The books of knowledge have been passed down from generation to generation, and more than once the Manchus have tried to take them. Many of my people died protecting the books, but none has ever been lost."

The old man paused. "None, that is, until three years ago."

"What happened, Mr. Ming?" Holmes asked.

"There is a man I once called brother. A man whom I trusted because we are of one blood. And, although we are the sons of different parents, we are both called Ming. The blood of Ming flows in our veins. By election of the family, my house was to keep the books of knowledge, and while Chang Tow seemed to accept it at the time, he never let go of his dream that one day Ming should again rule China.

"About three years ago, Chang Tow came to my house with an Englishman. I brought them into my home as guests and assumed that the Englishman knew nothing, as we are forbidden to speak of the books of knowledge to anyone outside the family."

"But we are not of your family," I remarked.

"That is true, Dr. Watson. It was hard for me to make this decision, but I have heard that you are men who can be trusted.

For you see, Chang Tow had told the Englishman of the books, and I have come to know that the Englishman had promised to help Chang regain the throne if Chang would, in turn, help him procure the mightiest book of all: the book of war."

Holmes's look was one I had seen before. And, although he did not speak, I could read the word in his eyes: Mephistopheles.

"Wu, my youngest, was the guardian of the books the day it was taken. He is here because it is his ultimate responsibility to return it to China. His brother Soong is here because he chooses to be. It is his right, as firstborn, to help his brother if he chooses. I am here to bring them both back to their mother alive.

"The Englishman and Chang Tow drugged my son and left my home that day, leaving no trace as to where they had gone. We have searched for them since then, and it was only about six months ago that we learned of Chang's diplomatic service in England. We have discovered much about his plans to blackmail your country with his great dragons. He needs the ransom to build more rockets and assemble an army."

"Tell me, sir," I asked, "if this book of war is so powerful, why didn't your ancestors use it to defeat the Manchus?"

"A good question, Dr. Watson. You see, the rulers believed that the secrets were so dangerous that they came to fear the knowledge itself. They forbade that the terrible weapons should be constructed, and so they relied on the old ways for protection. But in the end the old ways were not enough."

"Let me ask you something, Mr. Ming." Holmes came alive again. "Chang Tow said that he was the one who gave the dragons their eyes to see and wings to fly, but that it was the Englishman who gave him the dragon's fire. Do you know what he meant by this?"

"I believe I do, Mr. Holmes. Chang was able to assemble his rockets based on the information he obtained from the book of war. But the formula for the special gunpowder is not a simple one. It requires very rare herbs which are not easily found. The powder must be ground very fine and then mixed with the proper quantities of the different herbs. But it appears that this Englishman is a clever man, indeed. For I have come to know that he has succeeded in supplying Chang Tow with the necessary materials. Chang knows a great deal about fireworks. As a young man he designed a means by which a rocket could be directed to its target, using a small, rotating wheel which fits into the rocket's tip."

"Mr. Ming," I spoke again, "you seem to know a bit more about all this than we do. Have you been able to determine the location of these so-called dragons?"

"Ah, give me a moment."

The old man stood and walked over to the fireplace. Taking a small wooden chest from the mantel, he opened it and produced a scroll of parchment. Returning to us, he handed it to me and bade me unroll it. There, painted on its surface, was a very extensive and complete map of England.

"Do you see the small dragons I have painted in," he explained, pointing with the stem of his pipe. "They represent the locations of two of the great rockets. Unfortunately, my sons and I have not yet been able to locate the third."

Holmes and I studied the paper carefully, with anxious eyes. It was then I noticed that one of the dragons appeared to be located a mile or so off the eastern seacoast, near the town of Southend-on-Sea.

"Is there an island here?" I asked Lee Ho.

"No, there is not," he said softly. "The rocket is nested in a watertight structure on the ocean floor."

"What!" I blurted, "how can that be?"

"Yes, Watson," Holmes interjected, "it is quite possible to build such a structure."

"The second dragon," Lee Ho continued, "is near the town of Aylesbury, in the country. But it is more heavily guarded than the other, and just as difficult to reach. For you see, it too is submerged."

"Submerged?" I puzzled.

"Yes, gentlemen, submerged beneath the ground. It will be no small feat to reach it."

"This information is extremely vital," said Holmes. "Is there anything else you can tell us, sir?"

"Only this, Mr. Holmes. Chang Tow is a very intelligent man. If you should make the slightest error in judgment, your

London will cease to be. I am sorry to say this, for he is Ming . . . as am I. And it is because of Ming that you know this grave danger. My sons and I will do everything in our power to help you overcome him. He must be stopped, and we must regain the book of war, as it also is our duty."

Just then, the clock on the mantel struck five.

"My sons must return you now. The sun is nearly upon us. Take this map with you, and should you wish to contact me, set two lamps on your roof in the evening."

"Thank you, Mr. Ming." Holmes shook the kindly Oriental's hand. "You have proven yourself a true friend."

With that, Soong and Wu led us back to the skyship, which was still anchored on the roof. We set off on the early morning breeze and arrived on the outskirts of London as the pink rays of first light peeked over the horizon. Fearing they would be spotted before they could return, the young men left us off on a lonesome road not far from the city. As we walked towards the familiar street lamps of London, Holmes began to apologize for the way things had gone that evening.

"Well, Watson, I failed to keep my promise to you. I assured you a good night's rest, and this has been the result."

"You needn't apologize, Holmes. You had no way of knowing we would be descended on by those fellows. Besides, the evening has proved quite profitable."

"It has, indeed, Watson."

My associate seemed more chipper now.

"If we can catch a cab quickly, we might be able to slip in another hour's sleep or so."

"It would be wonderful, Holmes. But if you don't mind, there's someone I'd like to see before we meet with Charlie this morning."

I spoke, of course, of Emily Cantaville. I so wanted to call on her that day, and it seemed that this might be my only opportunity, considering the information we had just obtained.

"Certainly, my friend." Holmes was polite but reserved. "I'll meet you at the Yard at eight o'clock."

"Eight o'clock, then," I said as we reached the cobblestone street.

My companion walked on as I sat down on the curb to rest my feet and wait for transport. Having a moment to reflect on the past few days, I mused about my associate as he disappeared in the distance. It seemed that whenever I spoke of Emily, or whenever Holmes was in her presence, his reactions were those of a man truly interested. But he spoke not a word about her, nor made any attempt to make his feelings known. Perhaps, I thought, he does not wish to challenge me for her, in any way, because of our close friendship. That would be like him. Or perhaps he is not really interested at all, and I only imagined it. That would be like me. But whatever the case, I was anxious to see Emily, and I'm confident that I woke half of London shouting down a cabby I had spotted a block or so away.

It turned out he lived nearby, but was reluctant to accept my fare because he had been out all evening and was ready for a little sleep himself. But I promised him something extra for his trouble and he finally agreed.

The trip to the address Emily had given me was a relatively short one, which was good fortune for my tender back.

I stepped to the street, handing the exhausted driver twice the fare.

"Thank you, gov'nor." His heavy eyes brightened now. "Should I wait 'ere?"

"No, thank you, cabby. Have a good day's rest."

As he drove off, I envied him the hot breakfast and warm bed that probably awaited him.

"Oh, well," I sighed, "there's always tonight."

Emily's home was a handsome one. It had belonged to her father and I was relieved that she had, at least, been able to retain the family residence.

I walked boldly to the door and rang the front bell. But after I had done so, I began to have second thoughts. It was quite early and she would surely still be in her bed. But a moment later the door opened, and there stood a rather large woman with a very stern face. She was dressed like a servant, and held a large iron skillet in her right hand as though it were a weapon.

"What do you want, sir!" she demanded.

"Ah . . . well," I muttered, taken aback by her ferocity. "My name is Dr. Johnathan Watson, and--"

The words had no more than left my mouth when suddenly Emily pushed her way past the belligerent woman and threw herself into my arms.

"Oh, Johnathan," she sobbed, "thank God you're here. It's all right, Maggy, he's a friend."

She was dressed in a blue full-length nightgown and was crying almost uncontrollably. It was obvious that she had been doing so for some time, as her eyes were red and nearly swollen shut.

"My dear, what is the matter?" I asked compassionately.

"Oh, Johnathan, he has taken Jeffry."

"Who has taken Jeffry?" I asked. "Who is Jeffry?"

"That man Ling. He and his men came and took him last night. He is my son."

Chapter Four

With that , Emily fainted.

"Bring her in quickly!" the feisty woman exclaimed.

I cradled her in my arms and carried her to the sofa, where I promptly checked for pulse and respiration.

"Leave her to me!" the woman scolded, still holding the large skillet.

"Madam!" I replied, a bit belligerent myself. "I am a doctor, and well able to care for Miss Cantaville. Now make yourself useful and bring a pitcher of cool water and a washcloth."

She paused, reluctant for a moment, but then conceded and left the room. An instant later, Emily moaned and opened her eyes.

"Oh, Johnathan, he's taken my Jeffry."

"You must relax, my dear." I did not want her to faint again. "Take a few deep breaths, and then we'll talk about it."

She did as I asked, wiping her tears with trembling hands.

"Let me sit up now, John."

Just then, the servant returned with the water.

"Perhaps you shouldn't get up yet," I said.

"No, I'm all right, now. I must be calm for Jeffry's sake. I must tell you what happened."

Composing herself admirably, Emily began by introducing me to her maid.

"This is Maggy, my dearest friend. When I could no longer afford to keep the servants, she stayed with us. Maggy was my nanny when I was a little girl, and has been with my family since before I was born."

"How do you do," I said, extending my hand to her.

"Very well, thank you," she replied gruffly, and then walked away, leaving my hand unshaken.

"Please don't mind Maggy, John. She's very protective and very untrusting of most men."

"Emily," I said softly, "tell me about your son."

She lowered her eyes for a moment, as though unable to find the words. But soon she held herself erect once more.

"Do you ever remember hearing of a man named Walter Penrod?"

"Well," I puzzled, "the name Penrod does sound familiar."

"When I was eighteen," she continued, "he had some business dealings with my father. He also had a son named Richard who would often accompany his father to our home. I, of course, entertained Richard with the usual outings, as was expected of a young girl in those days.

"He was older than I and very handsome. But he had a terrible temper and was given to hard drinking on occasion. One day, when he and his father came to visit, we went for a picnic in the country. While we were there, he asked me to marry him. I told him that I was very flattered to be asked, but I was not ready for such an important decision in my life. At first he seemed to accept my answer gracefully, but he drank heavily all that afternoon. And as he did, he became more angry and abusive with each drink. When I demanded that he bring me home, he suddenly became enraged, and then . . ."

She paused now, and a single tear ran down her soft cheek.

"And then he forced himself on me."

"Oh, my dear." I took her hand. "I had no idea."

"Afterwards he hated himself for what he had done. He wept and begged me, on his knees, to forgive him. He pleaded with me not to reveal his crime. And so I agreed to remain silent, on the condition that he would never see me again. And from then on, whenever his father came to our home, he came alone.

"It was only a few months later that Richard was killed in a duel. I suppose his bad temper had gotten the best of him. But my problems were not over."

She paused again.

"You were with child," I whispered.

"Yes!" she sobbed. "I refused to believe it at first. But it's not the sort of thing you can deny for long.

76

"When I discovered the truth, I went to my father and told him everything. He was very angry with me for not telling him right away. But then he realized my misfortune, and arranged for me to stay with friends in Londsbury. I went there to have my baby, and my father arranged to have the child taken in by another family. I was to return to London afterwards as though nothing had happened. But . . ."

She began to cry again.

"But you fell in love with your baby. Didn't you?" I said softly.

"Yes. I couldn't give him up and I couldn't bring him home. I stayed in Londsbury, and although Father was upset in the beginning, he came to love Jeffry, too. I have such fond memories of my father's visits with us. He would bring gifts when he came, and I would laugh when he made silly faces for Jeffry. We were so happy for a while.

"But after Father died, I decided to return home, to London. My brother and I told everyone that Jeffry was our infant cousin whose mother had died and left him to my care. It went well for a while, but eventually the truth came out. And then my poor brother had such terrible financial problems. We were rejected by the rest of the family, and poor Freddy lost all hope. '

"After he died, I was left alone with Jeffry and sweet Maggy, who had remained with us despite everything. I had to let the other servants go. I couldn't afford them. But I was determined to raise my son and provide for him, whatever the cost."

She stood now, and turned her back to me.

"I had very little money left. And it seemed for a while that I would even lose this house. But I was not about to let that happen."

She turned towards me with a cold expression.

"I did what I had to do to provide for my son."

It was evident to me that she was thoroughly ashamed of her questionable means of support, but she had been hardened by the long years of struggle.

"Emily," I said with compassion, "I do not judge you. Please, let me help you in any way I can."

Her eyes softened then, and she extended her hands to me.

"Find my son, John. Bring him back to me. He's all that matters to me now."

"What time was he taken?" I asked, moved by her desperate plea.

"They came about two o'clock last night. They were very silent, and could have left without my knowing. But that horrible man, Ling, came into my room and woke me. He told me he was taking Jeffry, and that he would bring him back after his work was complete. I was terribly frightened, and I begged him not to take my Jeffry. But he just smiled at me and said nothing more. Then he left."

"All right, then," I said with determination. "Go and dress quickly. We'll bring this to Charlie and Holmes immediately. And, by all means, take courage, my dear. We'll find your son."

She smiled and rushed off to her room to change, while I went out to the street to hail us a cab. I believe it was then that I first realized how hopelessly in love with her I had become.

Before long we were racing through the city streets. I had given the cabby an outrageous fare to rush us to Scotland Yard as swiftly as his horse could manage.

We arrived in short order and hurried up to the briefing room where the meeting had been the previous evening. It was still early, but I knew that Holmes and Charlie would be there, anxious to begin the day.

When we entered the room, Holmes took one look at Emily and immediately sensed that something was amiss.

"What is it, Watson? What's wrong?"

"Let's all take a seat," I suggested. "There's much to be told."

Holmes had already briefed Charlie on our strange meeting with Lee Ho and his sons that night. So while the Yard's experts examined the parchment map that Lee Ho had given us, I explained the tragedy that had befallen Emily that same evening. As I spoke, the inspector seemed glass-eyed and distant, but Holmes was as attentive as ever, and I again noticed a strangeness in his manner as he watched Emily, who was struggling to keep her composure.

". . . and that is all she can tell us," I concluded.

"Well, gentlemen," Holmes remarked, "it would seem Mr. Ling is taking every precaution to insure that we do not interfere with his plans."

"I'm afraid so," Charlie agreed. "I'm so sorry that you became involved with all this, Miss Cantaville. We will, of course, do everything in our power to try and find your son."

"Thank you, Inspector," Emily said softly. "I know you will do all you can."

The inspector then turned his attention back to Holmes. "Can you contact this Lee Ho fellow and arrange another meeting with him?"

"Yes, Inspector, I do have a way of reaching him."

"Well, Holmes, please do so. I think the sooner we can come together on this matter, the better."

"What about the boy?" I asked anxiously, as Charlie had seemed to me less concerned than I had anticipated.

"Not to worry, Watson." He smiled and winked an eye. "I'll get some of my best men on it."

Satisfied, I let the subject go, for Charlie appeared to be most sincere. But there was something about his reaction to the entire matter that did not seem right.

We continued on with the meeting, and finally decided to set the signal lamps on the roof of our apartment that evening. Charlie would come and spend the night with us, in the event that our new allies should arrive in short order.

I must confess I did not look much forward to having the inspector as a house guest. Granted, he was a likeable enough chap, but he tended to get a bit windy when indulging in idle chit-chat.

After the briefing that morning, I took Emily home and begged her to take to her bed for some rest. She had had very little sleep the night before, and I was concerned for her health.

Fearing she would be restless, I left her a mild sedative and tried to alleviate some of her fear by babbling on about my associate's ability to find anyone, anywhere. She seemed encouraged and, in turn, sought to comfort me by insisting she would be fine, and that I should try to get some sleep myself.

Reluctantly, I left her and decided to return to our apartment for whatever sleep I could manage.

When I arrived home, Holmes was nowhere to be found. For a moment I thought about going out for a little breakfast, but discarded the idea for the sake of popping right into my bed.

Ten glorious hours later, the sound of voices downstairs awoke me. It was hard to believe that I could have slept for so long without interruption, considering the way the last few days had been. I rose quickly and threw on a robe and walked to the stairway to see if I could make out who it was I had heard in the sitting-room.

"Holmes, is that you?"

"Yes, Watson! Charlie has arrived and I've ordered in a bit of dinner. Why don't you come down and join us?"

"Sounds wonderful, old man. I'll be there in an instant."

Dressing quickly, I ran down to the study where Charlie and Holmes were now chatting. The sleep had been refreshing, and the food Holmes had ordered in was absolutely grand. In fact, it was so good that even Charlie's rambling on didn't bother me.

"I say, Holmes, did you get any rest today?"

"Yes, Watson, I did manage a few hours this afternoon. That is, when your snoring wasn't shaking the floor."

My associated laughed now, and we all enjoyed the joke.

"Well, Holmes, shouldn't we be getting the lamps on the roof?"

"Already done, Watson. All we can do now is wait."

We settled into the chairs and talked about anything and everything. It was an entertaining evening and a relatively peaceful one--that is, until Charlie brought us back to the realities at hand.

"Watson, I hope you will understand what I am about to say," the inspector said as he lit his pipe. "You must realize that the issue of Miss Cantaville's son must be considered secondary to the matter of Ling's threat."

I paused for a moment, not sure of Charlie's meaning.

"What are you saying, Charlie? What do you mean, secondary?"

"Watson," Holmes began, "I think--"

"No," I interrupted, "let him speak for himself, Holmes. What do you mean, secondary, Inspector?"

"Well, old man," Charlie began in a rather pompous tone, "the simple truth is, we must concentrate all our available manpower on the Ling case. Once we've been able to stabilize the situation, we can then turn our attention to--"

"So that's your game, is it!" I stood, enraged. "All that talk about putting your best men on the case, that was just a load of rubbish, wasn't it?"

"Watson, I believe--"

"No, Holmes, don't try to defend him! I've had my fill of this pompous ass, and I do not intend to stand idly by while Emily's son is in the hands of this villain. If you haven't the stomach for it, Inspector, I suggest you find someone else, besides me, to help you with this matter."

In great anger, I stormed towards the door to leave.

"Watson, sit down!" Holmes called in a stern voice of command.

I turned and looked at my colleague with rebellious eyes.

"Watson, please." His voice was quieter now, almost pleading. "Just take a moment and think. The lives of a million people are at stake here. If we make a move to rescue Emily's son, the sons and daughters of London will pay the price. I'm not saying we'll forsake the boy, but we must first be sure that this threat can be neutralized."

Holmes's words hit me hard. I knew he was right; but how would I tell Emily that her son was considered secondary? I took a moment to calm myself, and then slowly returned to my chair.

The inspector sat quiet for a short while, and then spoke.

"I'm sorry, John. I should have given your feelings more consideration."

"It's all right, Charlie," I replied. "Please forgive my insult."

"Already forgotten, old fellow."

It was not the first time I had called Charlie a pompous ass, and it probably wouldn't be the last. But he was quick to forgive, and got back to the business at hand.

"I should fill you in on the meetings I attended today."

"Oh, yes, Inspector." Holmes's eyebrows raised. "Have you had the opportunity to speak with Field Marshal Atkins?"

Charlie scowled. "I have indeed, and I must say he was not very pleased that Her Majesty has placed me over him."

"Are you so surprised, Charlie?" Holmes smiled. "After all, the field marshal is accustomed to giving orders, not taking them."

The inspector just shrugged his shoulders and let the matter drop. He then proceeded to inform us about every minute of conversation he had engaged in that day. It wasn't long before we were all snoring, as even Charlie succumbed to the dull drone of his conversation.

I believe it was about four in the morning when a soft voice roused us from our slumber.

"Good evening, gentlemen."

The voice was that of Lee Ho, who was standing in the doorway of the study.

"Please come in, sir," Holmes invited as he rubbed the sleep from his eyes.

"Mr. Ming," Holmes continued, "this is Inspector Charles Whittington of Scotland Yard."

Charlie was a bit fuzzy yet, but he collected himself quickly and stood to greet our guest.

"Good evening to you, sir. I have many questions that I would like to ask."

"I hope I have the answers you desire," the small man answered.

We pulled the chairs round and began discussing the affair at length. When Holmes told Lee Ho about the kidnapping incident, the old man lowered his eyes and sighed deeply.

"I am greatly dishonored," he began. "Chang Tow has become a man driven by his lust for power. My family is shamed by his actions. You must believe me when I tell you he was not always this way. When we were young, Chang saved my life. One day, when we were in the country together, I fell on my knife and hurt myself badly. Chang carried me several miles on his back to reach help."

His face became even sadder now.

"He was so very good then. But now . . . he is the dragon. And I am forced to become his enemy."

"Mr. Ming," Holmes said softly, "do you have any hint as to where the third rocket might be?"

"I am sorry, gentlemen. I'm afraid I do not."

"How were you able to discover the locations of the other two rockets?" Charlie asked.

"We were able to make contact with a member of our family who was working with Chang Tow here in England. I convinced him that Chang's intentions were evil, and that no good thing could come from this. I also persuaded him to give us whatever information he could about the locations of the rockets, and the whereabouts of the book of war. He was able to tell me where two of the dragons were nested, as he had helped to place them there. But before he could discover the location of the third dragon, or find the book of war . . ."

He paused as though his heart was too heavy to continue.

"He said that Chang was very secretive about these, and that it would be difficult to keep trying, until one day in winter . . . one day in winter we found him dead in the snow. Chang had found out about him somehow." Tears welled in the old man's eyes. "Ming has killed Ming. And now I must stop the dragon from killing all of you. Which means that I am forced to set myself against him."

We remained silent for a short time, not wanting to prod the poor man at so painful a moment. But we needed his information, and were compelled to continue our questioning.

"How difficult would it be to make a successful assault on the rocket locations without prompting a launch?" Holmes asked.

"Very difficult indeed," he answered. "The rocket near Southend-on-Sea is about one mile offshore and several feet below the surface of the water. It is contained in a structure that is large enough to house a small guard of about ten men. They live in this underwater fortress continually, although sometimes a few of them must come in for necessary supplies."

"And how is this done?" I asked.

"By means of an underwater boat which allows them to move to shore undetected."

"Amazing!" Holmes exclaimed. "How are they able to keep their air fresh in such places?"

"The book of war contains many secrets. It would be nearly impossible to approach them without being seen."

"What about the rocket near Aylesbury?" Charlie inquired.

"The rocket there is deep in the ground. The fortress is larger than the other and has a guard of about twenty men. Its entrance is located on a small but steeply sloping hill with no trees or brush for cover. It, too, would be almost impossible to reach without being discovered."

Holmes sat silent for a moment, and I could see that he was deep in thought. He then rose from his chair and walked to the fireplace to light a pipe. Turning towards us once more, he drew a few puffs and then revealed his conjecture.

"It would seem that Mr. Ling has been very careful to keep his dragons spread well apart. This is, of course, advantageous against the advent of an assault, as he could still carry out his threat on London even if he lost two of his rockets. A single rocket could set the entire city ablaze. But the great distances between them must surely make communications difficult. I imagine he must rely on telegraph or messenger to stay in contact with his people."

"You are quite right, Mr. Holmes," Lee Ho replied. "We have discovered that a telegraph message is sent to Dover from each location every three days."

"And messengers?" Charlie asked anxiously.

"None that I know of."

"Well, that may be an advantage for us," Holmes mused.

"But a telegraph message must be received every three days," I insisted. "If we disturb either of the locations, Ling will surely come to know it."

"Not necessarily, Watson," Holmes replied. "It may be possible to strike at all three locations simultaneously --that is, if we can locate the third dragon."

"Yes, I believe you may have something there, Holmes." Charlie's eyes became bright. "Three small assault teams of crack troops could possibly carry out such a maneuver."

"But the problem remains, gentlemen," said I. "We still have no idea where the third rocket might be, not to mention the difficulty of reaching the locations we're already aware of without being seen."

"One thing at a time, Watson," Holmes remarked as he approached Lee Ho. "We've still the best part of a month left to find out where the third rocket could be. Do you think you might be able to contact another family member in Ling's ranks who would consider defecting?"

"I have tried," the old man answered, "but in doing so, I revealed my presence here in England to Chang Tow. And since then, he has been careful to watch his men closely."

"Would you consider trying again?" Charlie asked.

"Yes, of course I will," the friendly Chinaman said as he stood. "But now I must leave you before the morning is come."

We said our good-byes to him as he returned to the roof where his sons were waiting. By this time we were too awake to think about sleeping, so we decided to plan our strategy for the coming day.

"Why don't I start assembling the strike teams," Charlie remarked. "I'll get with Field Marshal Atkins, and we can handpick the best men that the army and the Yard have to offer."

"An excellent idea, Inspector," Holmes agreed. "In the meantime, Watson and I will do a little legwork. I looked into something yesterday that may prove helpful."

With that, Charlie gathered his things and made for the door. "I'll check back with you this evening," he said. "I want to get back to the Yard and start going through personnel files."

"Very good then, Charlie," Holmes called. "You may wish to notify the London Museum as well. I'm sure that Ling will try to steal the Ming artifacts before the month is out."

"Right you are," Charlie answered as he walked off into the damp morning.

"Well, Holmes," I said, shutting the door, "what bit of information were you able to come up with yesterday?"

"While you were sleeping so soundly, Watson, I went to see Willy."

"Willy? Has he found something?"

"Surely, Watson, you realize that there is no one in London who can come or go without being noticed by someone?"

"What are you trying to say, old man?" I squinted, not getting the point.

"I know where Miss Cantaville's son is being held."

"What!" I blurted, overwhelmed with surprise. "How did you find out?"

"When we returned from Dover, I took the precaution of having Miss Cantaville watched by a few of Willy's people."

My associate now turned away from me, as though hiding something his face might reveal.

"I was concerned that she might have seen or heard something in her dealings with Mr. Ling that would cause him to move against her. But apparently this was not the case. If she had gained any crucial information, Ling would surely have taken her and not the boy. I believe his kidnapping Jeffry was a move to insure our cooperation in meeting his demands without further interference."

"But where did they take him?"

"To Dover, Watson, probably Morlock Castle."

"Well, then, what are we waiting for! Let's find passage to Dover."

Holmes now turned towards me once more. His face was somber but steady, and his eyes met mine firmly.

"I know you don't want to hear this now, my friend, but Charlie was right. We dare not try to rescue Jeffry until we have neutralized all of Ling's rockets. The risk is too great."

I saw my associate draw back within himself, the way he always does when we're about to have a disagreement. But this time his intuition failed him. For I knew that, although my heart was telling me otherwise, this was how it had to be.

"Well, then," I said plainly. "I suppose it's time we went dragon-hunting."

"Right you are, Watson!" Holmes answered, encouraged by the way I had handled it all. "Take heart, my friend. We'll have this Ling fellow for supper one day soon."

We set out that day in search of anything that might lead us to the third rocket. But the next three weeks proved to be disappointing ones, at best. In that time we had met, on and off again, with Charlie, Field Marshal Atkins, and Lee Ho. But our progress was slow, and each new lead left us empty-handed. There seemed to be no cracking the impenetrable wall of security that Ling had set up around his operation.

Finally with little more than a week left before the next full moon, Holmes called an emergency meeting to discuss the necessity of immediate action.

The meeting was to be held at Wellingshire Castle, for Lee Ho had indicated to us that he had been able to obtain another bit of information from Ling's ranks. It was agreed that the meeting would begin at midnight, and so I decided to take advantage of the early evening and pay a short visit to Emily.

I had stopped to see her frequently in the past few weeks, and did all I could to comfort her. But it was difficult being near her; knowing what I knew about Jeffry's whereabouts, and not be able to say anything. It was hard for me because my feelings for Emily were growing stronger, and the whole possibility of London's complete destruction seemed more and more likely with each passing day.

I had taken my dinner that evening in a shop not far from the Cantaville home. It was only a few blocks away, so I decided to walk. Nearing her home, my heart began pounding rapidly, which served to remind me that my feelings for her would be all the more difficult to hide. But then, I thought, why should I hide them? She already knows I care for her.

I made up my mind then and there to ask her that very evening to be my wife.

As I rounded the corner, the front of the Cantaville home came into view. But to my great surprise, I saw Emily standing on the front step with a man. A man that looked familiar. It was Holmes.

I stood motionless for a moment, not knowing what to make of it. But then I reasoned that surely my friend was there for the same reason as I, to comfort this poor woman in her time of distress.

Suddenly she reached out and embraced him, kissing him with such passion that it caused my heart to sink like a stone.

I could not have been more crushed. Not only had I been betrayed by Emily, but by my dearest friend as well.

A moment later Holmes said good-bye and walked away as she waved from the step. After she returned to the house I waited a few minutes, not knowing what to do. I then gathered as much courage as I could muster and walked to her door. I just stood there, trying to find the strength to ring the bell.

She must have spotted me from the window, because a moment later she opened the door.

"Hello, Johnathan," she said sweetly, "please come in."

"Oh . . . oh, no, I mustn't. Ah . . . I've an important meeting this evening. I . . . just stopped to see if you were all right."

"Oh, John, you are so caring. Please come in for a moment."

"Oh . . . no, I can't. I'm sorry."

I suppose Emily noticed that I really wasn't myself, and she questioned me about it.

"John, is something the matter?"

"No, my dear," I barked almost too loudly, "really, everything is going quite well."

"I know," she smiled. "I'm so fortunate to have you and Mr. Holmes looking for my Jeffry."

"Oh, yes!" I said. "Not to worry about that, we're hot on the trail."

"Well, thank you, John. Thank you with all my heart," she said cheerfully. It was then that we heard a high-pitched whistle. "Oh, the teakettle. Maggy's gone shopping. I'll have to get it. Please stay for one cup."

"No . . . thank you . . . I really must go."

Almost leaping from the step I walked off quickly, but she soon called after me.

"Take care of yourself, Johnathan. I'll be waiting to hear from you."

"Yes," I said, "don't worry about a thing."

It was a rather sorry walk back to Baker Street that evening. I thought about all the years Holmes and I had spent together, and how in all that time he had never once let me down in any way. I thought about Emily and how very much I loved her. But now, it seemed she had given her love to another.

The more I walked and thought about it, the more angry I became. How could they be so cruel and uncaring towards me? How could they cast me off so lightly?

By the time our apartment came into view, I had produced a full head of steam and was ready to unleash it upon my associate. I moved forward, spouting like a steam engine, my teeth grinding in fury.

It was at that moment, out of the corner of my eye, that I spied my reflection in the large sitting-room window of our building. The sight of my taut face and clenched fists stopped me dead in my tracks and prompted me to speak my disappointment aloud.

"You fool. You sorry fool. Who are you that these two should give some explanation for their actions? What hold do you have on this woman?"

It was obvious to me that there was only one thing I could do. Stand aside. Say nothing. And let my friends do as they will. It was surely the proper thing to do.

I entered our home and found Holmes in the study going over a few ideas he'd been working on. He looked up when he heard me, and smiled a warm hello.

"Good to see you, Watson. Did you have a pleasant dinner?"

"Yes, thank you, Holmes."

Glancing at the clock on the mantle, I noticed it was getting late.

"We'd best be going soon. We don't want to be late."

"Right you are, Watson. The coach should be here shortly."

Our ride did arrive within moments, and we sped off through the night towards Wellingshire Castle. I'm afraid I was much too quiet for my usual self that evening, and my associate was quick to pick it up.

"Is something troubling you, Watson? I don't mean to pry, but you seem preoccupied."

"Oh, no," I answered, trying to cover my sullen mood. "I'm really quite fine. But it does seem that Mr. Ling has us between the devil and the deep blue sea."

Holmes paused for an instant before speaking. "I know it looks bad for now, my friend. But take heart. Perhaps Lee Ho's new information will open a door."

"I hope you're right, Holmes," I said with a forced grin.

We reached our destination and were quickly led to the furnished sub-chamber. Present were Field Marshal Atkins, Inspector Whittington, Lee Ho and his sons, and, of course, Holmes and myself. As we settled into our chairs, Soong and Wu served tea and saw to it that everyone was made comfortable. Field Marshal Atkins was the first to address our small assembly.

"I must say, gentlemen, you've certainly found the deepest pit in England to have this chat."

He then looked a bit sheepishly at our host. "Sorry, old man. I know this is your temporary home."

"No offense taken, sir," Lee Ho remarked softly.

Holmes leaned towards the kindly Oriental and got right to the purpose of the meeting. "What have you found for us, Mr. Ming?"

Straightening himself in his chair, he took a small sip from his cup. "I'm afraid the news is not good. Since we were unable to contact another family member, my sons and I concentrated on seeking someone who could be bribed."

"And did you find that someone?" Holmes asked.

"Yes, we did." He looked at us woefully. "The man has told me that Chang plans to launch his dragons on the first night of the full moon."

"To launch if the ransom is not paid?" Inspector Whittington inquired.

"To launch whether the ransom is paid or not," Lee Ho answered.

"I knew it!" Holmes erupted. "This man has made up his mind to make an example of London to the rest of the world. There is no dealing with this fellow."

"Yes, I quite agree," the field marshal volunteered. "The man has no scruples whatsoever."

"What are we to do, then?" I asked in frustration. "We've only a week or so left, and we still have no idea where the third rocket might be hidden."

My associate then stood and walked to the center of our small circle. He lifted his head slowly and leveled a serious gaze to the group.

"I have a proposal to make, gentlemen. I believe it is the only avenue open to us now. I propose that we have no choice but to attack the two rocket locations that we know of, and hope that in the process we can discover the whereabouts of the third rocket placement. If we are fortunate, we may be able to find someone, or something, that will give us the information we need."

The field marshal wagged his head and moaned in an unsettled tone, "Sounds risky, old fellow."

"But if we don't try," I spoke in support of my friend, "Ling will destroy London anyway. What have we to lose?"

"You're right, Holmes," Charlie said, nodding in agreement. "You're absolutely right. It's the only chance we have. We must take the risk."

The meeting continued at great length, but it was finally decided that one small specialized assault force would be assembled. An attack would be launched on each rocket location individually, thus allowing us to concentrate all our energies in one spot. Once inside, we could move to overcome the guard, disable the rocket, and then seek for some clue of the last dragon's location.

It was also decided that any telegraph communications from the installations would have to be duplicated in order to assure that Ling would not become aware of our actions.

Holmes spoke again.

"One more thing, gentlemen." My associate's expression was hard. "No one must escape. If even one man should slip

91

away from us, it will mean the death sentence for London. On this matter there will be no margin for error."

We then set ourselves to the task of selecting the men for our small assault group. Seven were chosen from Scotland Yard, eight from the military. Their talents ranged from explosives expert to infiltration specialist to marksman. Lee Ho and his sons would be with us as consultants on Chinese weaponry, and also to aid us in the disarming of the rockets. Holmes, Charlie, Field Marshal Atkins and I would complete the list.

Because of the shortage of time, it was agreed that we would assemble and equip our small band at Scotland Yard in the morning and set out for Southend-on-Sea as early as possible. Southend-on-Sea was chosen for the first assault because of the relatively small guard which protected it, and also for the British naval presence nearby which could be called upon, should extra support become necessary.

The following morning we grouped together in the large munitions room of Scotland Yard. Each man was supplied with whatever weapon or tool he felt was needed to perform his particular task. Shortly thereafter, Field Marshal Atkins spread a large map of the seacoast on the floor and asked us all to gather round.

"This, gentlemen, is our target," he said, pointing with a riding crop. "We will soon be boarding a train that has been placed at our disposal for the sole purpose of this mission. It will take us all morning to reach Milford station. Once night falls, we will be riding horses to Southend-on-Sea, and you must be able to carry all your materials on horseback.

"When we reach the channel, we will reassess the situation and decide then if we wish to make any changes in the assault plan. If you have any questions, please hold them until we get on the train. Inspector Whittington and I will make ourselves available then. Since time is of the essence, gentlemen, we must leave immediately."

Minutes later, our train went streaking out of Chesterfield station at full throttle. We were all collected in three carriages, which were pulled by a huge, powerful engine that hurled us along at a fantastic speed.

Charlie had used his full authority to assure that all other traffic was cleared from our path, and that experienced workmen would be stationed along the way to provide us the swiftest service possible in the event of any breakdown.

Despite the obvious danger of the task that lay ahead, our spirits were high. Holmes was particularly happy because it was his plan of assault that was to be used, although he had convinced Charlie and Atkins it was their own.

I could hear the excitement in his voice as he confirmed the details with Lee Ho.

"Now, you're sure the entrance is here?"

"Yes, Mr. Holmes. It is constructed to look like a large warning float. Ships stay clear, as they are given to believe that there is a sandbar there."

"But this is not the case?"

"No, not at all," he replied. "You will notice that it does not move with the waves. The entrance is supported by a long, hollow tube which extends downward to the structure on the ocean floor. The tube has a dual purpose. It is used to bring fresh air down to the men inside, and also--that is, if we are unsuccessful--it will be used to launch the rocket."

"God forbid," I mumbled, as Holmes continued his questions.

"The underwater boat they use, must they enter and exit it from the surface?"

"No, it is not necessary," he explained. "It can be entered from their submerged fortress by means of an air-trapping chamber."

I suddenly shuddered. "That means that someone could escape with the underwater boat while we are entering by the surface tube."

"That is true, Dr. Watson. There is always that measure of risk."

The old Chinaman left us to rejoin his sons.

Holmes and I sat silent, contemplating the conflict that was to take place that evening. But at that moment, the picture of Holmes kissing Emily came into my head, and I knew I had to push it out of my mind.

Looking out the window, I could see a few dark clouds, which caused me to wonder about the weather conditions we might experience. The channel could be a nasty place in foul weather, but we could ill afford the luxury of waiting for conditions to improve.

I thought about Holmes's plan and couldn't help but wonder how well it could possibly work. We would have to approach the entrance of the underwater fortress with three small boats in total darkness. There would be no light that evening save for the moonlight, that could reveal our presence if there were no cloud cover at all.

The rumble of the wheels beneath us and the gentle swaying of the carriage soon lulled me to sleep. It was a peaceful slumber, and the morning's nap was refreshing.

Startled awake by a jolt from the brakes, I checked my watch and noted it was 11:20 a.m. as we finally pulled into Milford station. From the window I could see our horses being held by a group of Atkins's army regulars. High-spirited animals with lean, muscular bodies, our mounts were some of the finest-looking horse flesh I had ever seen.

We spent the afternoon and most of the early evening rehashing the details of the assault plan over and over. But when sundown arrived, we gathered our materials and, within a few short minutes, were riding off towards the sea.

Less than an hour later, we were galloping along the beach of Southend-on-Sea, where we found the boats that Atkins had arranged to have hidden in a large clump of brush just above the sand line, near the launching point we had chosen. The field marshal had wired ahead to make sure that they would be placed in precisely the right spot.

"Let's get them in the water and get moving," Charlie said anxiously.

His haste was understandable. The three-quarter moon was covered by clouds, but the sea was still relatively calm. There was no telling how long it might last, so it seemed best that we should act swiftly.

Suddenly the young Chinaman, Wu, cried out what sounded like a warning.

"What is it?" Holmes asked Lee Ho, who was just getting into one of the boats. "What's wrong?"

"My son has spotted something in the water coming this way. I think it is best that we hide ourselves until we can determine what it might be."

"Inspector!" Holmes called. "Get the men back on the beach and find cover!"

Deserting the boats, we scurried towards the brush and hid ourselves there. Only moments after we had done so, a hazy shape in the water, about eighty yards out, became visible to me.

It appeared to be a strange craft of some type, that looked very much like a large fish. Only the top half protruded from the water, and its skin was a metallic color, although somewhat rusted. The vessel was obviously some kind of ironclad boat.

Lee Ho was laying beside me. He whispered in the softest of voices, "It is the undersea boat. This may be a stroke of good fortune. I only hope they do not see our ships."

"What should we do?" I asked.

"We must capture it and use it to our advantage."

It was then that a small door opened on the top of the odd-looking craft, and two men emerged. As they waded towards us, I signaled to Holmes who nodded back in acknowledgement. He then passed it along to the rest of the men, and we waited in silence as they drew closer. We wanted to make sure they were close enough so that a retreat to their ship would be impossible.

Suddenly Field Marshal Atkins called the charge, and we were upon them in an instant. We had them greatly outnumbered, so the battle was a short one.

In the meantime, Lee Ho's sons had entered the underwater craft and pulled a third man from inside.

"Tie them up quickly!" Atkins barked. "Lieutenant Tompkins, remain here and stand guard. The rest of you come along." The field marshal smiled triumphantly. "We've just blocked their only escape route."

"Charlie! Field Marshal Atkins!" Holmes called.

They ran over together.

"What is it, Holmes?" Charlie asked, breathless.

"Lee Ho tells me that he and his sons can operate this vessel. Watson and I could join them and enter the fortress from underneath while you and the men come from above."

The field marshal's eyes became bright as he contemplated Holmes's plan. "Yes, what a wonderful idea. We'll enter both ways and catch them in the middle."

"Mr. Holmes," Lee Ho interrupted, "these men must surely have been coming in for supplies, but in a few days another telegraph message must be sent from the village."

"Yes, I am aware of that, my friend." Holmes looked at the old man with kind eyes. "We must locate the telegraph codes at all cost. But for now, gentlemen, I suggest we carry on with the assault while the sea is still calm."

"Right you are!" Charlie blurted in an excited tone.

With that, the men took to the boats while Lee Ho, his sons, and Holmes and I boarded the strange fishlike craft. It was a bit crowded inside, for the vessel had really been designed for four men and a modest amount of cargo. But the five of us settled in and made ourselves comfortable as best we could.

The interior of the remarkable craft was disquieting, to say the least. It was dimly lit by a small, glowing orb fastened to the ceiling above. The orb seemed to have no source of power and did not appear to be using any means of combustion.

"A sun crystal," Lee Ho whispered with a smile. He had noticed my intense curiosity about it.

"A sun crystal?" I puzzled. "What on earth is that?"

"It is a rare stone found only in certain parts of China. If you cut and polish it properly, and then set it in the sun for a few days, it will glow with a bright light for a long period. This crystal has faded with time, and is probably due to be replaced."

"Indeed," I answered. "Most astounding!"

He then turned and set his attentions on the panel in front of him, which was filled with levers and pull-ropes of all sorts. This, I assumed, was the control panel, and I could make out that each device was labeled with Chinese markings of some type.

At that moment there was a hissing sound, and the craft began to move.

"Could it be steam?" I whispered to my associate.

96

"I don't believe so, Watson. It sounds more like the noise we heard in the skyship."

Glancing to my right, I noticed a small porthole which gave me a view of the sea and the sky above. The channel still seemed relatively calm, and the cloud cover appeared adequate to hide the assault team's approach. I could see the men in the boats heading out. It was about then that we heard another hissing sound, and we could sense that the ship was starting to submerge.

As the water line moved up the porthole, I was suddenly taken by a moment of panic. I broke out in a cold sweat, and could feel my heart pounding within me like a steam hammer.

"Ah . . . Holmes," I stammered, "I'm finding it a bit difficult to breathe."

"Oh, dear," my associate replied. "I was afraid something like this might happen."

He examined my eyes and sweaty palms, and then smiled reassuringly. "Not to worry, Watson, I've just the thing for you right here." Holmes turned away from me briefly, and then swung around quickly, slapping me sternly across the face.

At first I was only stunned, but then my amazement turned to anger.

"I say, old man, what did you do that for!"

"How do you feel, Watson?" he asked.

"How do I feel! My face hurts, that's how I feel!"

"Good," Holmes remarked, as he suddenly swung another blow, this time meeting me soundly on the opposite side.

"Blast it, Holmes!" I roared, "what's gotten into you!"

"How do you feel now?" he asked again.

"Like going seven rounds with you, old boy! Does that answer your question?"

"Yes," he laughed, "I believe it does. But what I mean is, how are your pulse and respiration?"

"Oh!" I answered in surprise, suddenly realizing the reason for my friend's strange behavior. "Oh . . . ah, yes, I see what you mean. I . . . ah, feel much better."

It was a bit embarrassing, being a physician and not having recognized my own hysteria. But while I felt in control again, my face was quite sore, and I was still somewhat angry.

Leaning toward Holmes, I tapped him on the shoulder. As he turned, I caught him sharply across his right side with a flat hand.

"Thank you, Holmes," I said with a smirk.

"You're quite welcome, Watson," he replied, as he rubbed his cheek and shook his head wryly.

As we continued to descend, I squinted through the small porthole to try and catch some glimpse of the underwater surroundings. But all was in darkness, and it seemed to me most impossible for anyone to navigate in such conditions.

"How does he know where he's going, Holmes?" I asked with considerable nervousness.

"I believe he is following that instrument on the panel," my friend answered, pointing to what appeared to be a large compass.

"But even with a compass it would seem a very difficult task," I insisted.

"To be sure, Watson. But I don't believe that's what it is. I think it is somehow fixed on the position of the underwater structure, and no matter how we may vary our course, it always indicates the proper direction."

The whole thing was quite beyond me, so I decided to just sit back and try to concentrate on preparing myself for the assault.

I drew my revolver and made sure it was well loaded. I had been fortunate enough to locate a smaller pistol, one more reminiscent of my lost Mildred; while it was not quite the same, it did feel a bit more comfortable than the Yard's standard issue.

We seemed to be taking the longest time to reach our destination, so my thoughts wandered off to Emily. How dreadful she must be feeling, and how I wished I could be at her side to comfort her. Or, perhaps it should be Holmes at her side. If their love had truly blossomed, she would need him in the days to come.

I decided then and there that I would do everything in my power to assure that nothing dreadful happened to my associate--

not just because he was my friend, but also because the woman I loved needed him.

It was at that moment that my attention returned to the tiny confinement of the ship, as Lee Ho signaled our approach to the sunken fortress.

"We will soon be entering the lower chamber, gentlemen. Once we are inside, my sons will leave the ship first to secure the area for us. When all is clear they will signal us to exit."

We had taken the coats from two of the captured men. And now, Soong and Wu struggled in the stingy space of the cabin to put them on.

The masquerade would be a difficult one, even for them. They would have to leave our craft and get close enough to subdue the guards in the docking chamber without being recognized. While this was unsettling enough, I began to dwell on the fact that Charlie was in charge of the entire operation. I kept trying to convince myself that, with men like Holmes and Atkins at his side, he could hardly go wrong. But what Holmes had said that night in the coach, about Charlie making the fatal error, kept coming back to haunt me.

"We are about to enter the fortress now, gentlemen," Lee Ho said in a remarkably calm voice.

Looking out the small porthole, I could still see nothing but darkness. But then there was the faintest hint of light above us. The light intensified as we rose, and suddenly we broke surface, having ascended into what appeared to be a large air chamber.

Peering out, I could see that the ceiling was dotted with sun crystals like the one that illuminated our vessel, only much larger.

Soong and Wu stood and opened the small door above our heads. A moment later, they scurried out and leapt to a narrow walkway located alongside. We held our breath and listened for sounds of a skirmish, not knowing what the two young men might be facing.

"God save the Queen," was what we heard. It was the all-clear signal that we had decided upon earlier.

Our luck was holding. The two Chinamen had found the chamber empty, and were working quickly to secure our craft to a nearby mooring.

We joined them soon after and made our way down the walkway to a landing where a large iron door was located. The door apparently led to the interior of the structure.

We could hear what sounded like large steam engines rumbling somewhere deep within.

"What do you make of that, Holmes?" I asked in apprehension.

"They are the pumping machines," Lee Ho volunteered. "They are used to bring fresh air from the surface and also to pump water out."

It was then that Holmes noticed the handle on the door begin to move. He tried to signal a warning, but an instant later the door swung open and a large Oriental fellow stepped in.

He was dressed all in black, and he looked at us with startled eyes.

I was sure that he would cry out at any moment, and our element of surprise would be lost. But in a wink, Soong stepped to my side and took me roughly by the arm. Glancing over, I could see that Lee Ho and Wu had done the same to Holmes. Lee Ho then shouted what sounded like orders to the intruder.

It suddenly came to me that they were attempting to pass themselves as guards by treating us as prisoners. This plan seemed doomed to failure, as the man would surely realize that Lee Ho and his sons were not of his small group. But to my surprise it caused him to pause for an instant, and a look of confusion appeared on his face.

An instant was all that Soong required, for without warning he leapt straight up into the air and kicked the bewildered Oriental square in the forehead, causing him to reel backward against the wall, where he slumped to the floor, quite unconscious.

"Good show!" I barked, amazed by the young man's speed and agility.

"Good show," Soong echoed with a broad smile. "God save the Queen."

But our elation was short-lived. Holmes put a finger to his lips to quiet us. He leaned an ear out the doorway, and paused as though he were trying to gather a specific sound.

"What do you hear, Watson?" he whispered, still listening intently.

"Only those pumps, Holmes. Why do you ask?"

"That's just the problem. The assault group should have been here by now. We should be hearing the sounds of conflict."

I pulled out my pocket watch and saw that things should, indeed, have been well under way.

"I see what you mean, Holmes. I wonder what's become of them."

It suddenly came to me that we could be left in the same sticky spot as that night in the Paris sewer when Bently cut off our reinforcements.

"Well, I'm afraid we can't wait for them," Holmes said gravely. "We must assume that they will either be here shortly, or are not coming at all."

Lee Ho drew a small scroll from his coat. "According to my information, the rocket is located in the uppermost chamber. The surface tube comes from above and leads directly to the rocket chamber. While the shaft was mainly constructed for launching the rocket, it is also connected to the pumps for ventilation purposes. I believe we can enter the tube from the pumping room and use this passageway to climb up to the upper chamber. That way we can avoid the hallways and reduce the risk of being seen."

"Sounds like just the thing," Holmes agreed.

We started to make our way down a narrow hall which, to our good fortune, was deserted. As we went, I could hear the pulsing of the large steam pumps growing ever louder. Eventually, we drew near to a small metal door, and Lee Ho motioned to us to remain silent. The pumps inside were sure to be manned by at least one watchman, and it was imperative that we take the guard by surprise.

We were about to burst in, when the sudden sound of approaching footsteps could be heard behind us. Someone was coming down the hall, so we moved back a few feet and slipped into an adjacent hallway to hide ourselves in the shadows.

Presently a guard passed us carrying a tray with what looked like the evening meal. This sparked an idea in Holmes, and he whispered something to Lee Ho. The clever Oriental smiled a mischievous smile, and began making a curious ticking sound by tapping the heel of his shoe against the wall. The guard turned when he heard it, and set down the tray. As he slowly peered around the corner, Soong and Wu landed devastating blows to the man, who went flat on his back, as cold as the first poor chap. We then took him by the ankles and dragged him into the hall.

A moment later we had stripped him of his clothing. This time it was Wu who would attempt the masquerade, for he was closer to a man's stature than his brother. I must say he looked convincing in the guard's black uniform, but it would still take a bit of luck to pass it off.

The young man seemed filled with confidence, though, as he took the tray and walked boldly to the door of the pumping room. He turned a large wheel located in the center of the hatch, and then entered, carrying the tray high while keeping his head low to hide his face. The rest of us crept forward to watch through the open doorway.

We could see only one guard within, and Wu approached him quietly. It appeared that he had glanced only briefly at our imposter, and then turned back to make some adjustment on one of the large engines.

But to our astonishment, Wu suddenly stepped on a shoelace and toppled head over heels, throwing food and dishes everywhere. The guard spun around and saw the young man's stunned face. Realizing that it was not one of his own group, the guard lunged viciously at Wu who was still struggling to get to his feet.

It was then that Holmes leapt through the door and snatched an unbroken plate from the floor. With a quick flick of his wrist, he sent it hurling towards the guard and caught him squarely between the eyes. Grabbing his face, the man fell to his knees as we rushed forward and pounced on him. We worked quickly to bind and gag him before he could cry out.

"I'll tell you this much, Holmes," I said, panting as I stooped to tie the man's ankles, "Charlie had better be in the rocket chamber by the time we get there, or I'll personally demand his resignation."

"Well, Watson," Holmes answered with a grin, "if he's not, you will at least have had the satisfaction of the last word."

Last, indeed, I thought. Probably the last words I would ever speak.

With that, we dragged our captive behind one of the engines along with the guard we'd left in the hallway and set to work prying off one of the curved metal panels that would give us access to the large surface tube.

We were able to remove one of the panels with a long metal rod which had been used by the guard to make valve adjustments on the great steam engines. It took about half an hour to remove the plate, but once done, Holmes poked his head inside the shaft in order to assess the feasibility of our plan.

"I believe it will do," my associate said from the hollow confines. "There are ridges in here that we can use like the rungs of a ladder."

"But who knows what we'll find up there?" I remarked.

"Take heart, Watson," Holmes reassured me. "If there was a guard of only ten men to begin with, the odds should be about even. We left three on the beach, one in the lower entrance chamber, and we've two in here. That leaves only four guards left."

It hadn't struck me before, but I had to concede that he was right.

Holmes was the first to enter the surface tube and begin the ascent. The rest of us followed soon after. Since the installation had been built on an underwater cliff, and because we had entered at such a great depth, it would be necessary for us to climb a good distance in order to reach the upper rooms that were located on the ocean floor above. We could see bright light above us, which was shining into the tube from a rather large opening. This, I assumed, was the rocket chamber. I strained my hearing to try to catch some hint of who, or what, might await us. But all that was perceivable was the constant pounding of heavy steam engines below.

As we neared the opening, my heart began to throb in rhythm with the great machines.

Holmes and I reached the top together and peered cautiously into the illuminated chamber.

The sight we beheld was absolutely magnificent. The grand room was every inch of fifty feet high, with sun crystals dotting the walls and ceiling. On one wall, a large circular porthole gave us a breathtaking view of the underwater seascape. And there was a grand staircase that ascended to an open walkway with several doors which, I assumed, led to the upper living quarters.

But the most remarkable sight of all was that of the mighty rocket itself. It stood majestically before us, its red skin shining in the unnatural light of the sun crystals. Painted on its surface was the image of a large, flying dragon that glared at us with a fearsome gaze. The rocket stood about forty feet high, and was mounted on a heavy platform with wheels for mobility. Four strong chains ran down from the nose tip to the platform, which were, apparently, used to stabilize the rocket until it was time for launch. The opening where we were rose above us the height of the chamber, leading me to deduce that we were, indeed, within the launching shaft itself.

I mused at how strange this dragon looked. It had three ridiculously small fins at the bottom and, instead of being pointed at the top, it tapered to a rounded peak, giving the rocket an almost bullet-like appearance. If it had not been for the fact that all this was constructed for so evil a purpose, it would have been a most beautiful spectacle to behold. But as it was, I was chilled to the bone at the thought of this dragon's terrible destructive power.

Looking to my associate, I could tell that he was absorbing every detail of the chamber.

"It seems deserted enough, Holmes. Should we go in?"

"Yes, Watson, I believe that would be in order."

We moved in slowly. Holmes was the first to enter, followed shortly by the rest of us. Once inside, we examined the room more thoroughly to make sure that we were, indeed, alone.

It was then that I noticed a large Chinese gong suspended from the ceiling, very near the seascape window. It had looked more like a great wall hanging when I had viewed it from the surface tube. But now I could see that it was set out from the wall, and hung about four feet off the floor. The images of three winged dragons were painted on its surface; their fierce heads pointing downward, as though they were about to pounce upon some unseen prey.

"What do you make of this?" I whispered to Lee Ho. "Could this be their alarm?"

"Perhaps," he answered. "Perhaps not. Either way, we had best not disturb it."

Needless to say I agreed with him, and moved on to inspect the large porthole.

I must confess that I was completely captivated by the beauty of the sea beyond. The light that came from the chamber illuminated the sea floor for a short distance and had attracted several fish. Great and small, they came to peer at me as I stood hypnotized by the astounding picture. They moved past the window in a graceful ballet, causing me to forget for an instant where I was, and the grave business we were about.

But the spell was broken a moment later when Wu, who was standing near a doorway on the far side of the chamber, signaled to his father.

"Someone is coming," the old man warned in a quiet voice.

With that, we rushed to hide ourselves behind two great support pillars, and were just able to conceal ourselves an instant before the guards entered. There were five in all, and they seemed quite unhurried as they walked casually towards the staircase on the facing wall. Their leisurely pace led me to deduce that our intrusion had not yet been discovered. But it unnerved me that there were five of them, for this made eleven men in all; one more than we had anticipated. Still, the odds seemed acceptable, and having them all together was a stroke of good fortune.

We waited until their backs were to us and then rushed them, taking the black-clad sentries completely by surprise. It was over in a matter of moments. Holmes and I held the men at gunpoint while Soong and Wu bound their arms to the large support pillars.

"By jove, Holmes!" I exclaimed happily, "I do believe we've pulled it off."

"It would seem so, Watson," he answered, with a slight tone of reservation in his voice.

"What's wrong, Holmes?" I questioned. We have them all now, and--"

"Drop your weapons and raise your hands in the air!"

I looked up, stunned, to see a lone figure standing on the walkway overhead. He held in his hand a large pistol which, from the looks of its immense size, could accurately be described as a small cannon. The man was discernibly Caucasian and, to my great surprise, was dressed as a British naval officer; an admiral to be precise.

"Please do as I say, gentlemen, or I shall have no alternative but to kill you."

I did as he requested, but my associate kept his pistol in hand.

"A pleasant good evening to you, Admiral Shelby," said Holmes. "I see you have not lost your interest in marine warfare. Although it would seem that your loyalties have been a bit altered."

Shelby? I thought. Yes, of course, Admiral Reginald Shelby. I suddenly remembered Holmes mentioning his name to me once.

"Perhaps you did not hear me, sir," the man cocked his head in an arrogant fashion. "I said, drop your pistol and raise your hands."

But Holmes still did not obey. "Don't you remember me, sir?" Holmes spoke in a friendly tone.

Good, I thought, perhaps my associate has had some positive relationship with this man in the past.

"Why, yes, I believe I do remember you," Shelby answered. "You're Sherlock Holmes."

"Yes, he is!" I exclaimed with hope, my arms still in the air.

"Yes, Sherlock Holmes, the man responsible for my disgrace," replied Shelby.

"Blast it, Holmes," I muttered under my breath, "don't you have any old <u>friends</u>?"

The whole of it came back to me now. Admiral Shelby had been forced out of Her Majesty's service by a scandal that involved the disappearance of a large amount of gold that was being transported by the navy. The facts in the case were inconclusive, so the admiral was given the option of retiring quietly to avoid the embarrassment of misconduct charges. But in essence he had been thrown out on his ear. This all because of a young detective named Sherlock Holmes who had discovered some link between him and the missing gold.

"How fortunate for me," Shelby remarked joyfully. "I shall now have the pleasure of killing you. Now, for the last time, sir, drop your weapon."

Holmes then took his pistol and leveled it at the large porthole in the wall.

"Fire your weapon, Admiral," my associate began, "and I will flood this entire structure."

"You'll what?" I blurted, my eyes wide with astonishment.

"Oh, come now, Mr. Holmes," Shelby laughed. "You really don't expect me to believe you're serious."

"I assure you, Admiral, that I am deadly serious. After all, what have I to lose? If I don't fire, you will kill us anyway. But if I do, we will all die together, and the rocket will be destroyed."

"You do have a point there, Mr. Holmes," Shelby mused with raised eyebrows. "That would surely displease my friend, Mr. Ling, who has trusted me to carry out this mission. But what to do?" He paused and became most serious. "Let us see, then, who has the least to lose."

With that, Shelby took aim at Holmes, and we heard a prodigious click as he drew the trigger.

I was sure the end had come, and I looked to my associate with compassion in my heart. I didn't want him to die and think that I was still angry with him, although at that moment I was furious.

A shot rang out, and I fell flat to the floor, confused, trying to decide whether to start swimming or rush to my friend who would surely be mortally wounded. But looking up, I saw that neither was the case. Shelby's pistol had fallen to the floor and he was down on one knee, clutching his right shoulder. Holmes's weapon was still trained on the porthole, and I knew that Lee Ho and his sons did not carry firearms.

It was then that one of Charlie's crack marksmen emerged from the surface tube, followed shortly by the inspector, the field marshal, and the rest of our assault group.

"Sorry to be so late, gentlemen," Atkins explained, "but we were delayed by heavy seas."

"You needn't apologize, Field Marshal," I sighed, rising to my feet, "it only nearly cost us our lives."

"Oh . . ." Atkins replied. "Oh, I really am quite sorry, chaps, but the wind picked up without notice and . . . well, just one of those things, I suppose."

"We have some searching to do," Holmes interrupted. "We must gather all the information possible: telegraph codes, time tables, whatever we can find; hopefully the location of the third rocket, if that information is, indeed, here."

"I believe I may know where we might begin our search," Lee Ho volunteered. "My informant mentioned a small vault in one of the chambers. Perhaps Admiral Shelby can tell us where it is."

Shelby was obviously reluctant to cooperate with our request. But one of the captured guards eventually succumbed to our questioning and revealed to us the vault's location.

The find proved significant, as we were able to secure Ling's telegraph codes, the schedule for the launch at this installation, and also the sight near Aylesbury, not to mention a detailed map of the Aylesbury rocket placement. But unfortunately we found nothing pertaining to the location of the third dragon or the book of war. Afterward we assembled once more in the rocket chamber.

"This is everything, Holmes," I was sorry to say. "I'm afraid there's nothing here that might indicate where the third sight might be. But this rocket, and the one in Aylesbury, are scheduled for launch in five days at precisely midnight."

"I guessed as much, Watson," my associate said plainly. "I'm sure the third rocket has the same time table. We might as well be going."

"What about that thing, Holmes?" Charlie remarked, pointing towards the great rocket.

"Well, I suppose it would be best to have your people set a charge with a delayed fuse. But, mind you, we'll need plenty of time to get away."

Atkins spoke now and seemed a bit timid.

"Well, you see, we had a bit of trouble with the wind and all . . . and what with the boats swamping so badly."

"What are you trying to say, Field Marshal?" Holmes prompted.

"Well, you see," Charlie now joined in, "the explosives packs were quite heavy and we needed to lighten the boats." The inspector, now at a loss for words, blurted in frustration, "We threw the blasted things overboard."

"Threw them overboard!" I shouted in disbelief.

"Yes, overboard," Atkins echoed. "It was that or turn back."

"You did the right thing, of course," Holmes said calmly. "After all, if you had not reached us when you did, we would most likely be dead now."

Realizing that I had spoken out of place, I conveyed my apologies to Charlie and the field marshal.

"Please forgive my shouting, gentlemen. It's this cursed temper of mine."

"Not a second thought," Atkins said with a smile. "We've come to know you by now, Watson."

We all had a small laugh, and I remember how wonderfully it broke the tension.

It was agreed that the rocket could not be left as it was, so we set to work discussing what options there might be to putting the large firework out of commission. Lee Ho began questioning one of the guards in the hope of gaining some new information about the workings of the rocket. So I took the opportunity to walk over and take one last look out the large porthole.

It seemed sad that this remarkable structure had to be destroyed. Looking down, I spied a long narrow box set against the wall. Opening it, I discovered a grand mallet, the handle of which was marked with the symbols of the three dragons. Deducing that it was for the gong which hung nearby, I decided to try it out. Walking over to it, I drew back the mallet, taking aim at the center of the large circle. But in an instant, one of the captured guards began shouting frantically in Chinese as though he had gone mad.

"Do not sound the gong, Dr. Watson," Lee Ho spoke swiftly, raising his hand to still my intention.

"Why in heaven's name not?" I asked.

"Because if you do, the rocket will fire."

"Oh," I said, lowering the mallet slowly, "that is a very good reason."

"By jove, you've done it, Watson," my associate proclaimed.

"No, I didn't Holmes. But I almost did."

"No, my friend, you don't understand," Holmes laughed. "Let me show you."

Using a small grapple, my associate tied a thin rope to one end and threw it towards the center of the ceiling where it caught fast in the support framework. He then tied the long mallet to the dangling end and drew it over to the wall opposite the gong. Judging the proper angle of the mallet's swing, he attached it to a decorative candleholder with a second small line which he wrapped once around the bottom of the candle.

"Now, gentlemen, when the candle burns to this point," Holmes indicated the spot with his finger, "the mallet will swing across the room and strike the gong. And then . . ."

I finished his sentence for him.

"And then the rocket fires, and that's that."

"Precisely, Watson, we'll just leave it chained to the platform."

"Good show, Holmes," Charlie voiced his agreement. "Now, let's set a match to it and be off."

We had gathered the prisoners together, and it took some time for all of us to make our way up the surface tube. But once there, we loaded into the boats and made for shore. The channel was still a bit rough, but the winds had calmed a little, making our row back to shore slightly faster than the assault team's trip out to the fortress.

We had no more than stepped out of the boats when we heard a deep rumbling sound emanating from the sea behind us. I turned just in time to see the dark channel turn from black to blood scarlet and then to fiery red, with a water spout that looked enormous even at our great distance. I could see the waters boil like some huge kettle left too long on the fire.

And then, as quickly as it had begun, the water spout returned to earth and the sea became quiet and dark once more. The rumbling sound diminished, and all we could hear were the waves lapping up onto the beach.

I smiled at my associate, for I knew that the assault plan had been his all along, even though he had convinced Charlie and Atkins that he was only following their lead. He seemed quite satisfied indeed as he gazed out over the channel. But then his brow suddenly wrinkled, and he cocked his head as though momentarily puzzled.

"What is it, Holmes?" I called, for I had seen that look before, and it surely meant trouble.

"Dodge it, Watson!" was his cry of warning. "Everyone run for the high ground."

I did not have to think twice about that phrase. Whenever Holmes used it, I was quick to move and hold my questions for later.

"Get the prisoners up the embankment!" Holmes shouted as we scurried to get off the sand and up the hill.

When most of us were nearly at the top, I turned quickly and caught sight of the danger my friend had spotted. There in the distance, approaching at remarkable speed, was what looked like a long, white line that rose above the sea a substantial height. It was then that I realized that the line was a wave of great proportion. It must have been at least thirty feet high, and it slammed onto the beach with a tremendous force, lifting our abandoned boats like matchwood and shattering them to splinters on the rocks below.

A few moments later the wave receded and the beach became still once more. It had left the shore swept clean, and we all stood in silence, awed by the unfathomable destructive power of this mighty dragon.

Holmes was the first to regain his composure. He quickly moved up and down the way counting heads to see if everyone had gotten clear. I knew how important it was that none of the prisoners should escape lest they warn Ling of our intrusion. And I was glad that no member of our assault team had been lost. But it shook me to my very core to think that two more rockets like the one we had just witnessed were still out there, poised to strike at the heart of our beloved London.

"And we've no idea where the third might be," I said aloud, hardly even realizing that I had spoken.

Charlie was also deeply moved by the spectacle, as he suddenly bolted from my side and ran over to Shelby who was seated with the other captives. Taking him firmly by the arm, the inspector pulled him to his feet and looked him dead in the face.

"Admiral Reginald Shelby," Charlie began, his eyes ablaze, "I hereby arrest you for treason, in the name of the Crown."

Chapter Five

We lost no time getting our prisoners off to Milford station. The trip back to London was a jubilant one, as we shared jokes and old war stories with one another all through the long night's ride.

It was first light when we finally reached the city, and I sensed that my associate was most anxious to reach home once more.

"There is someone I really must visit before we leave for Aylesbury, Watson."

"Certainly, my friend," I said, realizing that he must surely be wanting to see Emily again before the next perilous assault. "I'll be going by our place for a hot bath and a change of clothes, and then meet you back here in a few hours."

"Oh, but Watson," Holmes exclaimed with some confusion, "I thought you'd come with me."

"Are you sure you want me along, old man?" I questioned in surprise. "I mean . . .wouldn't you rather go alone?"

"Of course not, Watson. I'm sure Finny would love to see you."

"Finny!" I said a bit too loud. "We're going to see Finny?"

"Yes, Watson. Who did you think?"

"Oh, never mind, Holmes, I just thought . . . well, never mind."

My associate looked at me a bit bewildered, but soon shrugged off my strange behavior. Stepping down from the carriage, he approached the field marshal who was busy instructing the head man of the engine crew.

"Now make sure she's ready by four o'clock this afternoon," Atkins barked. "We must be ready to pull out at four o'clock sharp."

The man only grunted a slight acknowledgement to the old soldier. After all, he was an employee of the train company, and was not accustomed to taking orders from a military man, much less one as gruff as Atkins.

"Field Marshal," Holmes called.

"Yes, what is it, old man?" He then shouted to the troops unloading the carriages. "Take those prisoners directly to Scotland Yard! Please, Holmes, I'm right in the thick of things, as you can see."

"I can tell you're quite occupied," my friend remarked, "but Watson and I have a bit of important business to attend to. We'll meet you back here this afternoon."

"Fine, fine," Atkins muttered, not bothering to turn his head, "but this train leaves for Aylesbury at four o'clock sharp, with you or without you."

"Right you are." Holmes smiled at me as we walked on. "The field marshal's a bit ragged this morning," he whispered. "I believe it must be his gout."

"Yes, indeed," I chuckled, "either that or he's still saddlesore."

With that, my friend threw back his head and laughed a hearty laugh. As we neared the platform where the cabs were waiting, Holmes walked over to the engine crew's head man and gave him a friendly good morning.

"I noticed that you had the pleasure of speaking with Field Marshal Atkins this morning."

The man just rolled his eyes and continued his work.

"Well, despite his growl, he's a rather good fellow." Holmes leaned over to him. "I think you should know there's an extra ten pounds for each of your men, and fifteen for you if she's fit and ready to roll by four o'clock this afternoon."

Suddenly the man's eyes brightened and a broad smile formed on his previously sullen face.

"Now you're talkin', gov'nor." He then stood and called to his crew, "Put your backs into it, lads! We've got a schedule to meet!"

Word of my friend's offer spread swiftly, and soon the large steam engine was covered with workmen, like ants swarming over a piece of sugar candy. There seemed little doubt that things would, indeed, be ready by that afternoon.

"Now I know why you're such a successful detective," I told him as we walked towards our cab.

114

"Why is that, Watson?" he asked.

"Because you're a scoundrel," I said gleefully, "and it takes a scoundrel to catch a scoundrel."

"I suppose you're right," he answered with a mischievous grin.

We found ourselves then, that morning, on the way to the home of a certain Mr. Thaddeus Finn--Finny, as we called him. A most unusual man. A man even more eccentric than my dear associate, and that is saying something.

Having great wealth, Finny had every opportunity to live like a king. But what did he choose? A large, old house in one of the most destitute parts of the city. He would often say that he preferred the people who lived there, and found that they were more tolerant of his way of life. Tolerant is the right word. For his bizarre experiments, at all hours of the night, often caused such a ruckus that the entire area could suddenly be sent into an uproar. But you see, this was not unusual in Finny's neighborhood. Actually, it was rather normal for that part of London.

He was often robbed, and no wonder. Finny never locked his doors, and was of the opinion that if someone took something from him, he probably needed it worse than him.

That was Finny. A brilliant scientist, really, with a great deal of heart, but too little sense, or so I perceived. In any event, it was always nice to see him again, as a visit with Finny was most assuredly never boring.

As our cab moved through the streets, I was suddenly shaken by a thought which rocked me to my very core.

"By jove, Holmes!" I shouted, startling my companion. "I have it!"

"What do you have, my dear Watson?" he asked, wide-eyed.

"I believe I have deduced the location of the third rocket."

"Have you, indeed," my associate remarked quite matter-of-factly. "By all means, please tell me."

"Holmes, do you remember the large gong we found in the underwater fortress, the one I almost sounded prematurely?"

"Yes, Watson," he acknowledged.

"I remember it clearly now, that day Ling held us at Morlock Castle. There was a Chinese gong in the throne room that looked just like the one we saw in the underwater fortress. Do you recall it?"

"Yes, my friend, I do," Holmes said while placing a consoling hand on my shoulder. "I remembered it the moment we saw the gong at South-on-Sea. Don't you see, Watson? He has laid a trail a blind man could follow. First he brought us to the castle. Then he took Miss Cantaville's son. And now there are the similar gongs. Don't you see? He would like nothing more than for us to believe that the third dragon is in Dover."

"But why would he lead us to his castle?" I puzzled.

"If he leads us to himself, he will know exactly what we're about. He would be able to determine the most opportune time for an assault on the museum. You know how badly he wants the Ming treasures."

I looked at my companion a bit sheepishly. "And I fell for it, all the way."

"Don't take it too hard, my friend," Holmes said warmly. "This dragon is a clever one."

"Well, where then," I asked in frustration, "is that blasted third rocket?"

"I'm not sure, Watson," he answered. "If Ling is not yet aware of our assault on his sea fortress, then he can't know that we have seen a second gong, so that shouldn't be part of his false trail. On the other hand, he may have even wanted us to capture at least one of his installations so he could throw us off the scent with false information about the other two locations, especially the third. Make no mistake, Watson, this one is quite a fox. That's sort of why I wanted to visit Finny. I'm hoping he can joggle my wits a bit."

It was then that we arrived at our destination. I settled up with the driver while Holmes climbed the steps to the front door.

"Why don't you wait here, Watson, and I'll see if he's home."

"Right you are," I told him, "the morning air might do me good."

My associate reached the door and let himself in. For, as always, it was unlocked, and there was little point to ringing the bell. If Finny were involved in one of his experiments, he wouldn't answer it anyway.

I looked around and studied the bleak surroundings about me. There were a few small children playing in the street just down the way from where I stood. They were dressed in little more than rags, and were smudged with dirt from head to toe. I could hear a woman crying somewhere, and the smell of raw sewage permeated the air.

"I cannot, for the life of me, see why he chooses to live in such a place," I said aloud.

But then a thought struck me. Finny said that these were his people. And, at least, he had the courage to make his home among them. He gave them his money, a place to stay if they needed one, and a compassionate ear, if nothing else. All I ever had given them was my pity, that noble emotion which eases the conscience but profits no one.

But my meditation was broken by a soft voice which came from the early morning shadows of a nearby alleyway.

"Mornin', gov'nor. Buy my sweet lavender?"

I looked up to see a young woman standing near Finny's front stairs, just outside the entrance to the alley. She was a young prostitute, overly dressed in an old, frilly evening gown, and reeking of stale perfume. But despite this, she was a pretty little thing with light hair and deep, blue eyes. I approached her slowly, and looked curiously into her soft, childlike face.

"What is your name, girl?" I asked.

"Well, love," she whispered in a provocative tone, "me friends calls me Flower."

"Tell me, Flower, how old are you? Sixteen? Seventeen?"

"I'll 'ave you know I was nineteen last month," she answered almost defensively.

"How old?" I pressed.

"Well," she began reluctantly, "I'm seventeen anyways."

"Tell me, do you have a husband?"

"'Course I do." She drew back now, unsure of my intentions. "Say, you ask a lot of questions. You a copper or somethin'?"

"Do you have a husband?" I insisted.

"I said, 'course I do. Well . . .I used to. 'E wasn't really me 'usband, just a friend. 'E run off a while ago."

She backed away then, as though she would leave. But I stepped to her side and blocked her exit.

"Do you have any children?"

"Say now, 'oo do you think you are, gov'nor?"

"Do you have any children?" I repeated. "It's a simple question."

"I got a baby boy, if it's any of your business."

"Do you like being a prostitute, young lady?"

"All right, that's it," she blurted, her voice full of panic. "You just let me pass right now or I'll call the coppers."

"You listen to me," I said, reaching into my pocket. "Here is twenty pounds. Take it and get passage for your baby and yourself to Maidstone. Do you know where it is?"

"Why . . .yes, I think so, sir," she answered in astonishment.

I then pulled out one of my calling cards and pressed it into her small hand.

"When you get to Maidstone, find a Doctor Robert Pullens, give him this, and tell him that I said he is to give you a job and a decent place to live. Do you understand?"

She seemed ever so startled. "I think so, sir."

An instant later she bolted past me towards the alley. But when she reached the entrance, she paused and turned only her head.

"God bless you, gov'nor," she whispered, and then disappeared into the morning shadows once more.

I just stood there wondering if she would really do as I had asked; or would she throw the money away on liquor and a jolly time? And what of her baby? How could I know? She reminded me so of Emily and her son; of how Emily, too, had fallen from grace because of desperate circumstances. And I wondered if God was watching over them, and if He cared for them, and all of us, for that matter, in these darkest of days. Surely He must, I thought.

"Come on in, Watson. Finny will see us now."

It was Holmes calling to me from the front door.

"Yes," I answered, collecting myself, "I'll be right there."

As I climbed the stairs to the front door, I couldn't get the vision of the young woman out of my head. At least she and her son, I thought, might escape the destruction that seemed more and more likely with each passing day.

When I entered the old house, I could hardly see my hand in front of my face. Finny always kept the place dimly lit, as he claimed that strong light hurt his eyes. The house was a huge old monstrosity with wide, drafty halls and large, unkept rooms. It was ten times the space that Finny really needed, and was in a state of mortal disrepair. Most of the rooms were cluttered with old furniture that was covered with molding dust cloths. It was not out of the ordinary to walk into a room and find some poor stranger nestled in a chair, sleeping off the hard drink of the night before. But that morning we were alone, with only the old dwelling's ghosts to keep us company.

As we entered Finny's study, it was plain to see that the strange old fellow was deeply absorbed in his work. A rustic-looking chap with long gray hair, he laughed to himself as he worked. And I observed him with great curiosity as he poured some sort of powder into a strange-looking apparatus on his work table. He was every bit of sixty now and, although his eyes were failing, he threw up his arms and chuckled when he saw us.

"Oh, Watson, you're here as well. How delightful. Now I can show you both."

"Show us what, Finny?" I asked.

"Why, my newest discovery, of course," he replied with glee.

With that, he ran over and embraced us happily.

"So wonderful to see you both again," he laughed, while reaching into the pocket of his baggy lab coat. "Here, put on these dark spectacles. You'll need them to protect your eyes."

"Ah . . . just a moment, Finny," I stammered. "The last time you showed us one of your discoveries, you ruined one of my best jackets."

"Oh, yes, Watson, I do remember that," he said. "Dreadfully sorry, old boy, but I did warn you not to startle the bird while it was on your shoulder."

He then uttered another small chuckle and returned to his work table. "Just a little more powder," he said, pouring a bit more of the substance into the object.

The device on his work table consisted of a round metal chamber with a long tube protruding out of it. The tube itself was pointed towards a thin metal plate which Finny had affixed to the table about three feet away from where the device was.

"There now," he proclaimed, "it's ready. Put on your spectacles, gentlemen."

I did so reluctantly, as did my associate.

"That's not gunpowder, is it, Finny?" I asked, a bit nervous.

"Not at all, Watson," he assured me. "It's just a little flash powder--well . . . actually . . . a lot of flash powder."

"Is it some sort of photograph?" Holmes inquired.

"You'll soon see," he said, reaching into his pocket once more and retrieving a match. "Here we go."

Striking the match on the table, he lit the end of a long fuse that extended out of the bulbous chamber of the strange apparatus.

"Oh, by the way," Finny remarked as he rejoined us near the doorway, "I should tell you that there may be the slightest chance of an explosion."

That was all Holmes and I needed to hear. Looking at each other with wide eyes, we bolted for an old, moldy sofa on the far side of the room and hid ourselves behind it. Finny himself was hot on our heels and quick to join us behind our hastily chosen barricade.

"Now, you must watch," he chuckled, putting on his own dark spectacles. "If you blink you'll miss it."

We kept our heads down, staying only as high as was needed to witness the experiment, and watched in apprehension as the fuse burned lower and lower. Finally it reached the powder.

What we saw then can only be described as absolutely remarkable. As a great billow of smoke erupted from the chamber, a single fine line of bright red light burst forth from the long tube and struck the metal plate dead center. It was all over in an instant, and Finny quickly leapt to his feet with a triumphant shout.

"You see! You see!" he blurted. "I have done it. Isn't it amazing!"

Holmes and I stood slowly, then walked with Finny over to the table to inspect the results. The air was filled with the foggy smoke from the flash powder, so I had to remove the dark spectacles to see where I was going. But once there, we found that the metal plate was completely unaltered, except for a tiny hole in the center which was still smoldering from the intense heat of the strange light beam.

"Isn't it wonderful, gentlemen?" Finny laughed with glee. "Have you ever seen anything like it? I call it ruby light."

"Ruby light?" Holmes questioned.

"Yes, ruby light. This long stem contains a rod of finely polished rubies which extends into this chamber and somehow intensifies the light from the flash powder."

I could see from his expression that my colleague was as fascinated by it as Finny. Holmes had a deep and abiding respect for the old eccentric. And while I was not entirely sure about the extent of their relationship, I did know that they had been friends for many years, and that Holmes had gained much of his scientific brilliance from working closely with Finny at one time.

"Yes, it's really something, old fellow," I remarked. "But tell me, what is its purpose?"

"Its purpose?" Finny echoed.

"Yes, what is it good for?"

"Well, it could be used . . . " He turned and cocked his head. "Well, all sorts of things, really. You could . . . and then there's . . ." The kindly old man paused for a moment and then blurted in frustration, "How do I know what it's good for? I've just discovered it!"

"It's really quite something, Finny," Holmes interrupted, and then put a warm hand on his shoulder. "But, my old friend, I need your advice. Could we talk for a few minutes?"

"Of course we can, Holmes," Finny answered, and then suddenly became very serious and subdued, not at all like the odd little man's typical manner.

Moving back to the large sofa, Holmes and I made ourselves comfortable while Finny pulled a chair over. He then looked at my associate with almost fatherly eyes and spoke in a soft, calm voice.

"Now tell me, lad, what is it you wanted to say?"

"Well, you see . . ." Holmes began, a bit unsure. "Let me see, how can I put it? Finny, if you were going to hide something from me, where would you hide it?"

"Oh, I would never try to hide anything from you, Sherly."

"Yes, Finny, I know," Holmes said with a warm smile. "But just assume for the moment that you did have something that you wanted to keep me from finding. Knowing me as you do, where would you stash it?"

"Well, I suppose . . . now let me think." He thought a bit longer. "Ah! I have it. If I had something I didn't want you to find, I'd hide it under your bed."

"Under my bed?" Holmes puzzled.

"Yes, you know, under your nose, as it were."

"He may just have something, Holmes," I remarked. "Lord knows you never look under your bed, much less consider cleaning there."

"That is an interesting thought," Holmes said with a sigh of disappointment, "but I don't believe a dragon would fit in so small a space."

"A dragon, you say?" Finny seemed quite curious.

"Never mind, Finny," Holmes replied. "Let me ask you this. Suppose you wanted to invade a fortress that was underground. The only way in that you knew of was a single shaft which was located at the top of a small hill. Now, mind you, there are no trees or brush for cover. How would you get in without being discovered?"

"Oh, that's quite simple," Finny said without hesitation. "I'd dig a tunnel."

"I see." My associate smiled. "But just suppose that there was no time to dig a tunnel. What if it had to be tonight?"

"Tonight!" Finny's eyes opened wide. "You mean this very night?"

"Yes, tonight."

"And there are no trees or brush for cover?"

"Not at all."

"My that does pose a problem." Finny scratched his head and closed his eyes. "Well, you could . . . no, no that wouldn't work. You might be able to . . . no, that wouldn't work either." He then wrinkled his brow and displayed a most unusual expression.

"What's he doing, Holmes?" I asked, a bit bewildered.

"He's thinking, Watson," was my friend's soft reply.

"Ah! I have it!" he cried, suddenly coming to life once more. "I fancy I would fly."

"Fly," said I plainly, with a tone of sarcasm. "Now why didn't I think of that?"

"No, Watson, really," insisted the old eccentric, who then stood and ran to his desk. Opening one of the drawers, he searched through some papers until he found what he was looking for. "Here are the plans. Do you remember the kite, Sherly?"

"Of course I do, Finny. I broke an ankle flying it once."

"That's right, you did," he chuckled. "Rather windy day as I recall. Nevertheless, it's probably the best way." He unfolded the paper and handed it to me. "Tell me, Holmes," he winked, "does the Yard still use those outdated chemicals."

"Yes, I believe they do," Holmes answered with a little wink of his own.

"Well then, I'll brew you up a batch of my new formula, and since you've no time to build your own kite, I'll lend you mine."

"Excuse me," I said, introducing myself back into the conversation, "but what in heaven's name are you two talking about?"

"Sleeping gas, Watson. Finny can brew up the necessary--"

123

"Just one moment," I interrupted. "Kites? Sleeping gas? Gentlemen, you can't be serious."

"Relax, Watson," my colleague reassured me, "it's Finny. You know he can be trusted."

"Trusted, yes, but relied upon? Hardly."

"Come, come, Watson," Finny cackled, "you know I'm a genius."

"Yes, Finny, but if it weren't for that fact, you'd be a blithering idiot."

Despite my reservations, I resolved myself to the reasoning that Finny's extraordinary plan was probably the only way into Ling's extraordinary fortress.

"It would seem that you've quite a desperate situation on your hands, gentlemen," the old fellow said now in a more somber tone.

"Yes, Finny," Holmes answered in a like manner, "it is a singular case indeed."

"Not to worry then, my friends," he said to cheer us. "I'll meet you at the train station at four o'clock with all the materials you will need. But remember, Sherly, you'll need a good, strong team of horses in order to reach the height you require."

"That will be no problem," Holmes told him as he shook his hand.

Finny then reached out and embraced him warmly, an act which I have known very few people to attempt with the most reserved Sherlock Holmes. "Be careful, my son. Come back to me soon." He then embraced me with the same vigor. "Watch after him, Watson," he whispered in my ear. "You know how little regard he has for his own safety."

"Ah, yes, Finny," I stammered aloud, "until we meet again."

We then said our good-byes and returned to the street. There didn't seem to be much traffic that day, so we decided to walk until we spotted a hansom.

"You know, Holmes," I said as we strolled, "I'm not sure what you're up to with this kite business, but whatever it is, I hope the inspector and Atkins will agree to it."

"Not to worry, Watson. I'll take care of Charlie and the good field marshal."

The general mood of the dreary neighborhood had brightened a bit as the morning sun peeked over the drab old buildings. It was then, to my great surprise, that I spotted Willy coming down the walk directly towards us.

"Look there, Holmes," I said, starting to point with a finger, "it's our man, Wil--"

"Put your hand down, Watson!" My associate spoke sharply. "Look straight ahead of you and, whatever happens, keep walking."

I did as he instructed and tried as best I could not to notice the familiar little man's approach. As we passed each other, Willy bumped into me, seemingly unintentionally.

"Oh, pardon me, gov'nor," he said as he brushed off the sleeve of my coat with his hand, "completely my fault."

He then walked on without another word, and I puzzled about it as the sound of his footsteps faded behind us.

"What was that all about?" I asked as we continued on.

"Wait until we round the corner, Watson, and I'll tell you."

Once we turned the corner, we kept up our pace, but my curiosity caused me to prod my companion again.

"What is it, Holmes?"

"Check the right-hand pocket of your coat, Watson. I fancy you'll find something there."

Reaching into the pocket, I came upon a small slip of paper. Pulling it out, I handed it to him and shook my head in remorse.

"Forgive me, old boy. I nearly gave Willy away. You'd think after all these years I'd be used to this sort of thing."

"It's all right, my friend," said he with understanding. "With what little sleep we've had, and all our comings and goings, it's a wonder that we've any reason left at all."

Reading the message quickly, Holmes suddenly stopped dead in his tracks, and looked to me with a startled expression.

"What is it, Holmes?" I asked with concern. For whenever Sherlock Holmes was startled, something was dreadfully wrong.

"Willy believes that Miss Cantaville's son has been moved to Aylesbury."

"Aylesbury! But why?"

"I don't know, Watson. Perhaps Ling has come to know of our assault of his water fortress. But there couldn't have been enough time to find it out. It could just be part of his original plan, nothing out of the ordinary. I'm not sure what to make of it."

"Nevertheless, Holmes," I said with a hint of panic in my voice, "we're heading for Aylesbury to hit that installation with all we've got. Emily's son will be caught right in the middle."

"Now take hold of yourself, Watson. If my plan works, odds are the boy will not be injured."

Sighing deeply, I calmed myself and looked to my associate.

"I do trust you, Holmes. If there's even the slightest hope for that poor boy, I know you're it. But I must tell, there are times when the entire situation appears to be absolutely hopeless to me."

His eyes filled with compassion, my companion took hold of my shoulders and gave me a determined gaze. "I will not let you down, my friend. Before the month is out, I promise you that Ling fellow's head on a platter."

What could I do but smile. Holmes was a man of very few promises to anyone, even me. But when he did, you could rest assured that he would allow nothing to stand in his way. He was many things, good and bad, but he was never a man given to failure.

"I know you, Holmes," I said happily. "When you set your mind to do something, not even the devil himself can stop you."

His eyebrows raised slowly.

"And that's exactly who we're dealing with," he said solemnly. "Willy believes that the boy has been taken to Aylesbury by the man I call Mephistopheles."

"Emily!" I shouted, suddenly remembering my promise to her. "We must tell her of this."

"That may not be wise, Watson."

"What do you mean, Holmes? We could at least tell her that we might know where the boy is; you know, give her a little hope."

"Well," said he reluctantly, "I suppose we could tell her that much. But we must be careful what we say. Ling's people could still be watching her."

"Of course," I agreed, "but let's find a cab while we've still some time left. We can stop by the apartment and change before we go back to the station."

We arrived at Emily's home shortly before noon. Holmes had convinced me to go to our apartment first so that we could spend the early afternoon with Emily, and then go directly to the train station. I was so excited about seeing her again that, for a short while, I forgot about her and Holmes. But when opened the door and I saw her beautiful, angelic face, it suddenly came back to me with unrelenting clarity.

"Johnathan! Mr. Holmes!" she squealed with delight, and then embraced us together. "You've found something more about Jeffry, haven't you? I can see it in your faces. Oh, please tell me."

"Let's go inside," Holmes said with a quiet voice, "and then we'll tell you what we know."

"Of course," she replied, wiping a tear from her glowing face. "Have you eaten yet, gentlemen? Maggy!" she called from the sitting-room. "Will you bring some tea and something to eat for our guests."

"Yes, dear," she answered, appearing briefly in the doorway. Even ill-tempered Maggy seemed excited by our visit.

"Do you have news of Jeffry?" Emily asked again as we seated ourselves.

"Yes, we do," I replied, a bit nervous, not sure how to conduct myself.

"Please tell me," she said clutching my hand.

"Well, we think he's been taken to Aylesbury. Although we're not completely sure. In any case, we're going there tonight and--"

"Ah, Watson," my associate interrupted. "I'm sorry, Miss Cantaville, but we're really not at liberty to speak of it in any detail."

"Of course," she said, "I understand, Mr. Holmes. But you do think there's a chance you might find Jeffry tonight?"

"Yes," Holmes replied reassuringly, "a reasonable possibility."

"Oh, I'm so encouraged," she cooed, embracing us once more. "I love you both so much, and I'm so grateful for all you're doing." Suddenly she bit her lip. And I could tell that she was fighting back an endless stream of a mother's tears. "So much for a five-year-old boy to endure."

It was then that Maggy came in with the tea, and we settled down to a quiet afternoon. The lunch was most delightful, and after my nervousness wore off I relaxed and enjoyed Emily's pleasant company. Holmes, too, seemed to let the tension go. He even napped a bit in a chair while Emily and I chatted about our families when we were children. The hours passed with such ease that I was startled when the clock in the corner chimed three.

"Oh, dear," I said, tapping my sleeping companion on the knee, "three o'clock, Holmes, we've got to be going."

"Is it already?" he popped up, blinking the sleep from his eyes and pulling his watch from his coat. "Why, so it is. Oh, Watson, would you mind if I had a brief word with Miss Cantaville in private?"

Holmes's request took me by surprise, but I did not want to make the situation awkward. So I forced a polite grin and made for the door quickly, turning my back before my true feelings could be detected.

"I'll get our ride and meet you out front," I said as I left.

It took only a few minutes to find a cab, so I sat down on the front steps to wait, all the while trying to convince myself that I was doing the right thing for Emily and Holmes by standing aside. Getting somewhat anxious because of the time and the distance we needed to travel, I returned to the house to prod my associate along. I let myself in and proceeded directly to the doorway of the sitting-room. It was then that I saw Emily embrace Holmes with the greatest of vigor, with what seemed to be the deepest of passion.

"I don't know what to say," she told him, "you've done so much for me."

Not wanting to be seen, I swiftly backed away from the doorway and hurried to the street.

"We'll be ready shortly," I told the cabby as I stepped inside the coach. It was a very difficult moment for me. My heart was breaking; and because they were the two people in the world I loved most, it was breaking all the more.

Presently Holmes and Emily came down to the street and said a cordial good-bye.

"Aren't you going to say good-bye to Miss Cantaville, Watson?" He spoke through the small window of the coach door.

"Oh, yes, of course, how rude of me," I replied.

Stepping to the walk, I shook her hand awkwardly and apologized for my lack of manners.

"Please forgive me, Emily. This past week has been most unsettling."

"I understand, John," she said, releasing my hand and hugging my neck warmly. "Take good care of yourself and remember that I'm thinking of you."

Her sweet fragrance and soft voice left me overwhelmed with emotion.

"My dear Emily," said I, my heart completely melted by her beauty, "you may count on me always, and always know that I will do everything in my power to see that you are happy."

"Thank you, John." She blushed. "All my hope and prayers go with you."

We then boarded our cab and left her standing on the curb as we sped off for the train station.

It was about a quarter to four when we arrived at the well-secured depot. Atkin's troops were everywhere, and the area around the train looked very much like a war zone. My associate's eyes rolled back in his head when he beheld the sight. He leapt from our cab before it had even come to a stop, and made a beeline for Atkins and Charlie who were standing near the engine.

"Hello, Holmes," Charlie called with a cheerful voice. "I believe we're all but ready to depart."

"Have you taken complete leave of your senses?" said Holmes angrily. "Where did all these extra men come from?"

"Now just a moment, sir--" Atkins began.

"Just a moment yourself," Holmes snapped back. "Are you trying to tell all of London what we're about? Don't you know that Ling's people could be anywhere? I'm surprised you didn't just take out an advertisement in the Times."

"Holmes, you're out of line," Charlie scolded.

"Like Hades I am!" my associate rebuffed the inspector. "And you both know I'm right. Now clear these men out of here immediately."

The inspector wrinkled his brow as though he would continue the argument, but Atkins, being a seasoned military strategist, at last conceded to Holmes.

"You're right, of course, old boy," the field marshal relented. "I should never have let Whittington talk me into moving the men from the museum."

"What!" my colleague shouted in utter amazement. "If there's one spot in London that Ling will strike at, it is surely there. The Ming artifacts may well be the only reason he has not yet destroyed the city. Surely he knows by now that his ransom demands will most probably not be met."

It was then that Charlie finally gave in to my friend.

"Blast it, Holmes, I suppose you're right," the inspector said, red-faced. "A few hours ago it seemed very reasonable to secure the station. But now it looks like we've made a mess of it."

Seeing Charlie's remorse, my associate calmed himself and spoke more respectfully to our old friend.

"Look, Charlie, I'm sure that it did seem like a good idea at the time, but I think you can see my point. How many men did you leave at the museum?"

"About seven," Atkins volunteered.

Holmes thought for a moment. "With the fifteen regular museum guards, that makes twenty-two men in all. Even if they were under attack right now, they should be able to hold out for an hour or so. How long ago did you pull the men?"

"About two hours ago," Atkins said as he looked at his watch.

"Then I suggest we get these extra people back to the museum as quickly as possible."

"Right you are," said Atkins, suddenly springing to life. "I just hope we didn't tip our hand to Ling."

It didn't take long for the field marshal to get his troops on the way. They were given orders to send back word immediately if the museum was, indeed, under siege. The rest of us set to work preparing ourselves for the journey to Aylesbury by gathering up the necessary materials and checking all the vital equipment. As we were loading the carriages, I noticed Holmes on the landing near the station house pacing with anxious anticipation. I knew that he was waiting for Finny to arrive with the materials we had discussed earlier, and it was already after four o'clock.

Suddenly he stood straight, his eyes fixed on something. He had spotted the good Mr. Finn seated atop a rickety old wagon near the entrance of the south gate. Finny had been stopped by one of Charlie's people who thought him a suspicious-looking fellow, and decided to question him. Bounding from the landing, my associate ran towards them calling, "Say there, let that man pass! Do you hear me!"

Seeing that it was Holmes who had shouted, the man stood aside and allowed Finny to enter.

"So sorry to be late," he called from the wagon. "The trip took much longer than I calculated."

"It's all right, Finny," Holmes replied, a bit breathless. "Pull your wagon over there and I'll see to having it unloaded."

Just then the inspector approached them and eyed Finny with a suspicious gaze of his own. "Who is this man, Holmes?" he asked.

"He's one of my people," Holmes answered. "He has some equipment here that needs to be loaded on board the train. We'll need it when we get to our destination."

Without a word more Charlie turned and walked away. He paused for just a moment to give instructions to three of the troops to help us, but then he continued on without so much as a slight glance backward. It was then that I perceived that Holmes's scolding had hurt Charlie's pride more than I had realized. His reaction was unsettling to me, so I mentioned it to my friend.

"Holmes, did you notice anything peculiar about Charlie?"

"Yes, Watson," he sighed. "I'm afraid I may have been a bit too hard on him. After all, the pressure he's under is tremendous. He's responsible for this entire operation, while at the same time he must struggle with the rest of us in the decision-making process."

We watched as the inspector continued his walk towards the engine; a lonely figure of a man, with what seemed to be the weight of the world on his shoulders. But what was done, was done. All we could do was load the materials on the train and get on board ourselves. Soon all was ready, and the engine master was given his signal. Thus we started out, bound for the peaceful English countryside near Aylesbury, bent on slaying the second of Ling's terrible dragons.

I started to settle in when I noticed Holmes standing near one of the windows. He was waving good-bye to Finny, who I observed from the window near where I was seated. The kindly old fellow was seated atop his wagon, and was waving and calling to Holmes with vigor. I saw in the old eccentric then, not so much the manner of a friend, but almost that of a father saying farewell to his son going off to war. And Holmes's typically reserved expression had now melted to that of a young boy's. His was the face of a child at that moment, and so I pretended not to notice them in so vulnerable an instant; a time when they both seemed to be remembering a very special past they had spent together which was, as yet, unknown to me.

After we left the station, my companion was quick to return to his normal reticent self. But as he came to join me, I couldn't help but remark about what I had observed.

"You love him like a father, don't you?"

"In many ways, Watson," he answered, realizing that I had seen, "he is my father."

I wasn't sure what to make of his remark, but I knew that this part of his life was deeply personal, so I did not pursue it further.

"Come with me, Watson," he said, checking the time. "We need to meet with Charlie and Atkins."

I knew why the meeting was necessary. It was imperative that they were told about the possibility of Emily's son being at the installation, and Holmes had yet to reveal his new plan for the assault. When we told them about Jeffry, Charlie was careful how he chose his words in my presence.

"Well . . . of course we'll do everything in our power to try and keep the boy from . . ."

"It's all right, Charlie," I said with quiet resolve. "I realize the possibility of disaster. We must do all we can to assure that the children of London are preserved." Then I bit my lip so hard that it bled. "And we must do this even if it means sacrificing the boy."

Neither Charlie nor Atkins commented on my statement. There was no need. They both knew I had come to accept the realities of the situation. But Holmes, sensing my despair, was quick to interrupt the silence.

"Gentlemen, I believe I have determined a plan by which we might neutralize the Aylesbury installation without injury to anyone--including Miss Cantaville's son."

Atkin's eyebrows raised. "Fill us in, old boy."

"It is really quite simple," Holmes began. "We have on board a large kite which can be pulled into the air by a strong team of horses. Once in the air, the kite can be maneuvered over the surface entrance of the fortress. Lee Ho has told me that the main entrance shaft is a bit larger than the one at Southend-on-Sea. Now this shaft is used for ventilation purposes as well as a launching tunnel. When the kite is directly above the opening, two glass containers of chemicals, which produce a potent sleeping gas, are then dropped into the shaft. The ventilation engines will circulate the gas in a matter of a few short minutes, so that, after a brief wait for it to dissipate, we can enter the fortress and secure it."

"Sounds remarkable, Holmes," I said, only now realizing the full scope of his plot. "But how will you know when the kite is directly over the shaft? And how will you release the containers?"

"Quite simple, Watson. I'll be riding on the kite."

His words took me by surprise. When he and Finny had spoken of it earlier, I didn't realize that the strange invention was meant to be manned.

"Now just a moment, Holmes," I protested. "I'm the first to admit that you're quite a clever fellow, but this seems so outrageous."

"Yes, Holmes," Atkins chimed in, "it hardly seems possible."

"But you don't understand," my associate said in defense of his idea. "I have flown this kite before. It's not as though it were untested."

"Tell me, sir," Charlie spoke with what almost sounded like contempt in his voice, "have you ever flown this kite at night? Are you sure the shaft will be visible from the air? Have you considered the possibility of being seen and giving us away?"

I could see that Charlie was well on his way to talking the field marshal out of my colleague's plan, and although I was not entirely sure of it myself, I had complete faith in my friend and was not about to allow the good inspector to succeed.

"I have an idea," I interrupted. "Let's see what Lee Ho thinks."

Atkins had one of his men summon the old man to us. When he arrived, Holmes explained his plan once more while we all sat in anticipation of his reaction.

"Yes," he said after a long pause, "it may well be the only way. Would the gas be harmful to us in any way?"

"No, not at all," Holmes reassured him, "nor will it harm those in the fortress. They will only sleep for about half an hour, but the gas will dissipate after a few short minutes so we may then enter and remain unaffected."

"Mr. Ling," Charlie said wryly, "your name is Ling, is it not?"

"Yes, it is, Inspector."

"And this Chang is a relative of yours?"

"Yes, he is my cousin."

"And you have no loyalties to him or--"

"Stop right there, Charlie," Holmes said sternly. "I don't like what you are implying."

134

"Nevertheless," Charlie insisted, "it is something that must be considered."

"I assure you, Inspector," Lee Ho spoke calmly, "you need not be concerned about my loyalties. I am committed to stopping Chang Tow from destroying your London, and to regaining our book of war."

"Do you believe, sir," Atkins asked, getting us away from the unpleasant subject, "that the shaft will be visible from the air?"

"Yes, there should be enough light coming from the chambers below to make it distinguishable from the air."

"But what are the odds he'll be spotted?" Charlie pressed the old Oriental.

"I do not believe the guards would be anticipating such an attack. I doubt that he would be seen, but there is always that risk. I assure you of this, you will never reach the entrance by land without being discovered. The area is thick with trip wires and traps of all kinds. Mr. Holmes's plan may not be entirely without fault, but I can think of no other alternative." He paused and looked directly at Charlie. "Can you, Inspector?"

Charlie did not answer, but it was evident that, in the absence of any other solution, Holmes's plan of assault would have to be adopted.

And so it was agreed that my associate would attempt to neutralize the Aylesbury fortress from the air, while we would wait at a safe distance for his signal. It was also established that no man must be allowed to escape, and that the secret telegraph codes and other vital information must be found.

"Remember," Holmes warned, "there is probably a back door somewhere. We must be watchful at all times. If word of our intrusion gets back to Ling . . ."

He did not finish his sentence, for we all knew what would happen if that were the case. We continued our discussion of my colleague's plan, but the calm of our small carriage was suddenly broken as two of the assault team's troops burst in with a man being forcibly held between them.

Thrashing with great vigor, the intruder was ridiculously small and slender. He was heavily dressed in a long winter coat, gentleman's cap and a woolen scarf he had wrapped tightly around his neck to mask his face. I thought it a wonder that the poor fellow was not smothering, considering the season, except that his entire apparel was baggy enough to allow some ventilation.

"We found this man hiding in the materials carriage ," one soldier reported to the field marshal. "We've no idea how he got there."

Holmes then squinted one eye and approached the strange captive. As he did, the man slowed his struggle and ultimately froze completely as though terrified. Slowly my associate began to unwrap the scarf which concealed the man's face. When he had finished, he stepped aside, revealing to all of us the stowaway's identity, the shock of which nearly knocked me from my feet. It was Emily.

"Good heavens!" Charlie shouted, jumping to his feet. "Unhand the woman!"

I could see that she had been perspiring heavily and was near fainting, probably more from her overheated condition than the shock. As the men released her, I rushed forward to support her once more while Holmes removed the heavy coat. Charlie opened a window and we seated her beside it, allowing her to catch a bit of the breeze.

"Emily," I said softly, "what in the world are you doing here?"

Just then, Atkins came over with a cup of water.

"Here you are, my dear."

"Thank you, sir," she replied, still a bit breathless. "Forgive me, John, I just had to come. When I heard that Jeffry might be where you were going, I couldn't help myself. Shortly after you left today, I changed quickly and came to the train station."

"But where did you get these clothes?" I asked.

"They were my brother's," she answered with a slight blush of embarrassment.

"Please tell me," the inspector asked anxiously, "how did you get on board the train, past all the guards?"

136

"It wasn't quite as difficult as I thought it would be," she said plainly. "I just waited until no one seemed to be watching and then slipped on."

The field marshal rolled his eyes. "Well, so much for our splendid security."

"Quite right," Charlie shook his head sadly. "It could have just as easily been one of Ling's people."

It was at that moment that Holmes returned to us from the front of the carriage where he had been speaking with our communications officer.

"Don't be too discouraged, Charlie," my associate reassured him. "We've just received word from London that the museum is still secure. No attempt has been made on the Ming artifacts. That being the case, we can reasonably assume that Ling is as yet unaware of our actions."

"Well, that's good news anyway," Charlie replied with a sigh of relief, and then turned his attentions to Emily. "My dear, you realize that I have no choice but to put you off at the next station?"

"Oh, Inspector, please," she implored him, "please let me go with you to Aylesbury. I promise I'll be no trouble."

"I'm sorry, my dear," he whispered apologetically, "but this train is no place for a woman."

"Charlie," Holmes spoke up, "I don't see the harm in her riding with us to Aylesbury. Once we arrive she can get a room in town, and Lord knows she'd be safer there than in London."

"Absolutely out of the question," Charlie snapped. "Sometimes I think you forget who is in charge of this operation, Mr. Holmes."

"Just a moment, Charlie," I said sternly. "You may be in charge, but yours is not the only voice here. We've agreed that we all have a say in these matters."

"And what say you?" the inspector turned to Field Marshal Atkins. "Would you have a woman on this trip?"

"Well, to be perfectly honest with you, old boy," the field marshal spoke without hesitation, "I really don't see the harm in it."

"Fine," Charlie answered bitterly, "have it as you like." He then stormed from the carriage without another word.

I remember that the incident had concerned me greatly, for it was the second time that day that we had locked horns with Charlie, and it seemed to be prying us apart at a time when our unity was crucial. Holmes, of course, was well aware of this, and was quick to follow the inspector.

"Don't worry, gentlemen, I'll talk to him."

Realizing that she had been the focus of our conflict, Emily looked to me with an uneasy gaze.

"I'm sorry, John. I didn't mean to cause you this."

"Not to worry, my dear," I said softly. "Charlie's a good man. He won't let this jeopardize our mission. Besides, I can understand your feelings for your son."

We sat quietly then, as she leaned her head on my shoulder to rest. The peaceful night and the gentle swaying of the carriage soon lulled her to sleep, but I found no rest on that uncertain eve. I sat there hour after hour just thinking; thinking about Emily and her son, Emily and Holmes, and a thousand other relationships and situations which were completely beyond my control. I suppose I would have gone on like that for countless hours more, except that my trance was broken by the piercing intrusion of a multitude of tiny bright dots. The images of distant lights. These were the lights of Aylesbury. And I could not help but wish that everything we had been through was just a bad dream; everything, that is, except Emily--to suddenly wake up and find that there was no Chang Ling, no dragons, no kidnapping of Emily's son. Only Emily herself at my side, with all the world at peace. But I knew that this was not so, for the distant lights grew brighter by the minute, and they served as a painful reminder of it all.

There were also other signs that we were nearing our destination. The activity in our carriage increased as different members of the assault team moved about collecting their equipment and checking their weapons. I looked up and spied Charlie walking towards us. He seemed calm now, and he spoke to me in a polite manner.

"We are nearing the city. When we reach Aylesbury, Watson, it will be at least an hour before we leave for the country. If you wish, you could help Miss Cantaville locate some lodging for the night."

"Thank you, Charlie," I said with gratitude. "I would like that very much."

He then addressed Emily, who was now awake. "Please forgive me, my dear, if I have offended you in any way. It's not that I minded your being with us. I was, quite frankly, concerned only for your safety."

"Thank you, Inspector," she said, smiling. "I know that you have a difficult job to do, and I was not the least bit offended by you earlier."

"Good-bye, then," Charlie said in a gentleman's tone, then left to rejoin Holmes and Atkins.

As we pulled into the station, the first thing that caught my eye was the long line of horses, like those we had at Southend-on-Sea, which had been prepared for our use by the military. But this time there were wagons as well, with gatling guns mounted on them. It was plain to see that a battle was about to take place, and I could not help but wonder what the outcome might be.

As the train came to an abrupt halt, we disembarked with the rest of our small band. And while Holmes and Charlie discussed the necessity of having the gatling guns along--useless noisemakers, as my companion put it--I spirited Emily away to the station house.

When we reached the landing, Emily clasped my arm firmly and pulled me to a stop.

"John, I'm going to find a cab and see myself into town. I know that you have to prepare for tonight and I won't keep you from it."

"Absolutely not," I insisted. "You'll need me to--"

"No, John!" she said with all the forcefulness of a tigress. "You must be prepared in order to defend yourself properly. You must be prepared if you are going to save my Jeffry. Please let me do this. I can care for myself quite well."

She was most beautiful to me at that moment. But I saw in her face a hardness that I had not seen since that day in Morlock Castle when she stood face to face with the villain, Ling, and fired a pistol at his arrogant head. And I suddenly recalled that she had taken care of her son and herself long before Holmes and I ever came along. But more than anything else, I saw before me a most courageous woman.

"All right," I conceded. "I think I understand."

"Good-bye, John," she said sweetly, and then kissed me deeply.

A moment later she was gone, and I just stood there puzzling on the matter.

Having seen Emily leave alone, Holmes approached me with a look of concern.

"Are you all right, my friend?" he asked gingerly.

"Confused as ever, thank you," I answered.

"Why is that, Watson?"

"Well, Holmes, I must admit that I have seen Emily kiss you. I wasn't going to say anything about it, but the kiss she just gave me seemed like that of a woman in love."

"Oh, my dear Watson. So that's why you've been acting so strangely. I can see that we are going to need to have a long chat."

He put a friendly hand on my shoulder and gave me a warm smile. "Come on, my friend, let's get ourselves ready."

We worked quickly to load all of our equipment into the wagons. Holmes asked Charlie to let him and me take one of the wagons so that we could discuss a little strategy on the way. But something told me that that was not what he had in mind.

Soon everything was ready, and it was about one o'clock in the morning when Atkins gave the signal to move out. The nearly full moon was alarmingly bright that evening; so bright, in fact, that we could see clearly in all directions for some distance. We had no more than started, when Charlie suddenly broke from the front of our small caravan and rode to our side.

"We'll have to keep our distance tonight. It will be easy to spot us. How close must we get in order to use the kite?"

"Well, Charlie," Holmes calculated, "I believe we can move to within one-quarter mile of the sight to unload. From there we can launch the kite, and the men can go on foot to surround the area to within a thousand feet or so of the entrance shaft. If you wait there for my signal, we should be able to converge on the entrance simultaneously."

"Yes, I see," Charlie said, nodding his agreement.

"But remember," Holmes added, "we had best leave a few fellows behind to guard against the advent of there being another exit. I know the plans we captured from Southend-on-Sea did not show any. But I find it hard to believe that there is no back door."

"Yes, not to worry," the inspector assured him, and then rode on to rejoin Atkins near the front of our group.

"I don't know, Watson," my associate said with a concerned tone. "I think I've been too hard on that fellow. He's just not himself."

"Oh, really," I remarked. "Well, Holmes, if Charlie's not himself, then who is he?"

"No, Watson, you know what I mean," he answered with a wry smile at my little joke. "He seems all right, but I sense something in him; something not like Charlie."

"Pay it no mind, Holmes," I told him. "Charlie's a good soldier. You know that. He'll do his job."

"Yes, I suppose you're right," he conceded.

But then he looked at me with different eyes, and took a deep breath as though he were searching for just the right words.

"Tell me, Watson, do you remember that day at the palace in the sitting-room when the queen called me over just before we left and whispered something to me?"

"Why, yes, I believe I do," I answered. "I'm still a bit green from envy."

"Well," he continued, "unbeknownst to anyone else, I had spoken to Her Majesty about the Ling problem even before I contacted Prime Minister Disraeli after our return from Morlock Castle. I informed her personally about Ling's ransom demands, and also the danger of his threat. But along with that, I asked her if she would inquire as to whether the treasury of England might still be in debt to a Mr. Windslow Cantaville.

"You see, Watson, in the panic of 1862, when it seemed that many of England's strongest and most established banks might fail, the treasury gave large loans to these banks. When it appeared that the treasury itself was about to go under, Queen Victoria sent out an urgent plea for help to the wealthiest of businessmen in our country. These businessmen, with their personal fortunes, supported the treasury of England and kept it afloat until the financial crisis had passed. But many of them, being men of great loyalty and devotion to the crown, had never asked repayment for their assistance. And although their credit is still on record, they simply refuse to collect. Windslow Cantaville was just such a man. But now his family is in crisis--I speak of Emily and her son--and it seemed only right that the debt should be repaid. That is what the queen whispered to me that evening in the sitting-room."

"Holmes," I interrupted, "are you saying that the government owes Emily money?"

"It would appear a great deal of money," he answered. "I wasn't sure at first how much, so I said nothing to you about the matter. When I told Miss Cantaville about it, she became very excited, but asked me to say nothing to you at that time."

"But why not?" I asked.

"Because, Watson, she knew how you felt about her, and she became afraid that, if things didn't work out, you would feel indebted to help her financially. You must remember that Miss Cantaville comes from a very proud family. She wanted your love, Watson, not your pity.

"But soon I found out that things looked very positive. When I went to tell her that day, she became very emotional and kissed me with excitement when she heard. This happened on her front steps and, as I recall, it was about then that you began acting strangely."

"Yes, Holmes, I saw it," I said sheepishly.

"I can only imagine what you must have thought, Watson. But you know Miss Cantaville. Every time I brought her more encouraging news, it was a hug or a kiss for me. It would seem that fate caused you to witness most of these displays of emotion."

"Oh, Holmes," I said with heartfelt remorse, "can you ever forgive me for what I thought?"

"There is no need to ask my forgiveness, my friend. What else could you think?"

"How much will Emily receive?"

"That hasn't been precisely determined yet," he told me, "but I found out it will most likely be quite a sum. I told her so, yesterday afternoon at her home and. . . ." he paused then and looked at me curiously. "Did you see that, too, Watson?"

"Yes," I said with great embarrassment. "I've been such a fool."

"No, you haven't, my friend," he said softly. "You've only acted like a man in love."

We said nothing more to each other after that, but remained silent, basking in the quiet warmth of our renewed friendship. And, despite the graveness of the task which lay ahead, the ride seemed light and easy that evening. For Holmes had restored my faith in him that night; a faith which he had never betrayed, but yet saw fit to confirm.

As our small band rounded a bend in the road, Atkins signaled us to move into a group of trees just off to the side. We brought our small caravan to rest there, and started to unload the wagons. As Holmes was assembling the kite, Charlie walked towards us with Atkins at his side.

"Where do you wish to set off from?" the inspector asked plainly.

"That long stretch of road we just traveled should be adequate," my associate answered. "I'll need a team of six horses for the wagon, and your best driver."

"You have it," Charlie replied, and then left us.

"I'm afraid the inspector is still a bit ruffled," Atkins said under his breath, not wanting Charlie to overhear. "I can't get more than a sentence or two out of him at one time."

"Yes, I know," Holmes remarked with concern. "Keep an eye on him, will you?"

"Right you are," Atkins assured him. "As for your driver, I'll get Phillips for you. He's by far the best we have. Just tell him what you want him to do."

"Thank you, Field Marshal," said I, as he left us to rejoin Charlie.

Holmes then set to work assembling the odd-looking contraption while I carefully removed the glass containers from their padded cartons.

"Be very careful with those, Watson," my colleague warned me. "If you drop them, we will end up sleeping through this assault."

I did as he recommended and gingerly set them on the grass. Looking up, I could see that he had quickly finished the strange aircraft and was carefully rechecking his work.

"What do you think, Watson?" he asked, holding the kite upright for my inspection.

Actually, I didn't know what to think. It looked very much like a large triangle about seven feet tall by five feet wide, and was covered with a leathery, thin cloth--like a bat's wing. The main frame of it had a support that extended out so as to allow enough space for a single passenger to slip into. Holmes then took hold of the support in order to show me how the kite was operated.

"You see, Watson, I will hold on here. This line will be my safety catch, for I will tie it to my belt before we launch off. The glass containers can be attached here, and here, on either side of my shoulders, so that I can release them at the proper moment. The main tow line is attached here in the front, and I will have to release it once I have reached my maximum altitude."

I must confess that it all looked very unfeasible to me at that moment.

"Holmes, are you sure you want to do this? Perhaps we could use some sort of camouflage and make our way to the shaft on the ground."

"In this bright moonlight, Watson? I expect we would arrive just in time to watch the rocket launch."

Sighing deeply, I conceded. "I catch your meaning," I said with quiet resolve.

Just then, Phillips pulled up with his team and wagon. Six of our strongest horses had been chosen for the task by Atkins himself, and the young officer who drove them was every bit as spirited as they.

"Do you want me to work them up slowly," he said to Holmes brightly, "or will you want a quick start?"

"When I give you the signal," my associate smiled, "you give them the devil."

"Yes, indeed, sir," the young soldier remarked with delight.

Holmes then spotted Charlie and ran over to him.

"Inspector, you can leave with the men now and get them into position. Have you chosen a few men to remain behind and guard the area? We don't want anyone slipping away."

"I've taken care of everything," Charlie answered, "not to worry, Holmes."

"Good, Charlie," Holmes said with a pat on his back. "I know we've had our differences, my friend, but we're quite the team, aren't we?"

Charlie's reaction to my colleague was a halfhearted smile. He then set to work assembling the men, while Holmes returned to our wagon.

"Let's move down the road and get ourselves ready," he said with a troubled wrinkle in his brow.

And so we did. As we pulled away from the others, Holmes called to the inspector.

"Remember, Charlie, I'll be going up at precisely two-thirty."

"Yes, two-thirty," he acknowledged, and then disappeared with the men into the woods nearby.

We went back in the direction from which we had come, and made our way down the long, straight road about a mile or so. When he felt the spot was right, Holmes told Phillips to turn the wagon around and stop. He and I then unloaded the materials and the kite. Tieing a rope to the back gate, my friend tested it with a few good pulls and then nodded that he was ready to begin. We walked down the road together, unraveling the line as we went, not speaking at all. Holmes carried the kite with one arm and held the coil of rope with the other, while I held fast to the two glass containers of sleeping gas, walking at his side with careful steps. When we reached the end of the rope, we were several yards away from our wagon. Holmes stopped here and tied the end of the line to the support bar of the kite.

"Now, Watson," he said while lashing himself to the support, "when I reach the proper height, I'll cut the rope and release myself. I will then guide the kite by shifting my weight from side to side. It should be a simple matter to spot the shaft entrance from up there. Even the slightest amount of light should be visible from that vantage point."

I then took the first glass container and started to fasten it to the support bar just beside his right shoulder.

"Please remember to be careful, Holmes," I said, as though I were his mother.

"Not to worry, Watson, the flight should be a simple one."

"It's not the flight that has me worried, my friend, it's your landing I'm concerned about."

He only smiled at my remark and said nothing more after that. I then took the second glass container and fastened it beside his left shoulder.

"There you are, Holmes," I said, a bit uneasy. "Not too late to change your mind."

"Why don't you join our driver, Watson?" he said, looking away into the distance. "It's very nearly time to go."

I remember how hard it was to simply turn and leave him.

"Holmes, I . . ."

"Please, Watson, no sentiment. There's really no time for it. If by some chance I don't make it, I'll meet you on the other side. Now go, my friend."

"See you soon, Sherlock," I blurted quickly, and then turned and ran towards the wagon. It was the first time in all the years I had known him that I called him by his first name. And although I had wanted to remain and tell him more, it was, indeed, very nearly time to go; not withstanding that the lump in my throat would not have allowed me to speak again anyway.

When I reached the wagon, I leapt aboard and seated myself beside our young driver. Looking at my watch, I could see that we were only a short while away from the half hour; although I had to wonder if the old time piece hadn't lost a few minutes, as was its usual temperament.

Suddenly, to my great surprise, Holmes called his signal loudly, and Phillips lashed the horses soundly, sending us hurling forward with a mighty jerk. Being unprepared, I was tossed head over heels onto the bed behind, but was able to right myself quickly in order to check on my companion. By the time I lifted my head upright, Holmes had already left the ground and was climbing into the night sky at a fantastic rate of speed. He waved his hand to let me know that he was all right, and I became so enthused that I cheered aloud.

It took very little time for him to reach his maximum height, for an instant later the line slackened and fell to the ground. Holmes had cut himself free and was now navigating the kite in the direction of the underground installation. I said a prayer of thanks at that moment, and also one for a safe journey for my companion. And I remembered how Finny had asked me to watch out for him, and wondered if I had somehow failed him by letting Holmes undertake so dangerous a task. But these thoughts left me quickly as I suddenly noticed that my associate was pulling away from us rapidly.

"Quickly, man!" I shouted to Phillips. "Get us to the meeting point."

With a crack of his whip and a sharp whistle, we lurched forward ever faster, speeding through the quiet night like madmen. As we moved in and out of the trees, I followed Holmes's flight as best I could, catching slight glimpses of him now and then. Suddenly the wagon began to slow, and I clenched my fist in frustration as my friend disappeared behind the trees once more.

"Sorry, Dr. Watson," the young officer said apologetically, "but we'll have to pull off and go on from here on foot. We can't risk being heard."

"Yes, you're right, of course," I sighed with disappointment. "But find a spot quickly so we can get started."

Pulling into a small clump of trees, we tied off the horses and started running in the direction of the shaft. I stumbled several times as we made our way through the dark countryside, for the sometimes thick canopy of the woods blocked out most of the bright moonlight. But despite these difficulties, I was still able to outrun Phillips and catch sight of my associate again. I observed that he was arcing his strange aircraft in a large circle, as it appeared that he had located his target and was getting himself into position for the strike. Realizing this, I increased my pace, while pressing a firm hand on my side in an attempt to quell the stitch I had developed. A moment later, a lone figure came streaking from the brush and wrestled me to the ground, causing us to land with a mighty thud.

"Planning on leading the charge, were you, Watson?"

It was Field Marshal Atkins. Without realizing it, I had reached the edge of the open field where the shaft was located and would have run dead onto it if my comrade had not stopped me.

"Sorry, old fellow," I said, quite out of breath. "Looks like I almost got us started ahead of schedule."

"It's all right, Doctor," he remarked with a wide smile. "As soon as we get Holmes's signal, we'll let you try again."

We then crawled together back into the brush and peered anxiously through the cover to observe my associate's daring attack.

What we beheld then was truly magnificent. Calculating the angle of his approach, Holmes made a sharp turn to the south, and then began to descend quickly, coming in low and fast for his strike. He reminded me very much of a falcon setting down upon its unsuspecting prey; a prey unaware of any danger, and completely unable to prevent its happening. He came at them no more than twenty feet above the ground, and we could see the canisters fall as he whisked past the confused guards who were keeping watch in the ground level opening. They were just inside, and had only spotted Holmes for the first time when he glided past a few feet above their heads.

We could hear their cries of warning to the others below, but it was to no avail. For my colleague had hit the mark, and soon their calls faded as they, too, like those down in the fortress, surrendered to the sleeping gas and toppled unconscious into the deep shaft. As my associate landed his craft, trotting to a swift halt, he waved at us to advance. And so we did, but with some care. For the surrounding field was thick with trip wires that were, fortunately, there only to sound an alarm within the underground fortress; an alarm which now no one was awake to hear. We reached the shaft quickly, and then counted heads to see if anyone had fallen prey to Ling's snares.

"Are we all here?" Atkins asked, looking about.

"Yes, the count is right," Charlie answered.

Just then, Holmes met us at the opening. "We will have to wait a few more minutes for the gas to dissipate," he cautioned.

"Good to see you, my friend." I smiled to him with great relief.

"And you also, Watson."

And then we embraced warmly, as though we had not seen each other in years. For in those few brief perilous minutes that we had just spent, we had lived a lifetime of concern for one another. And so we knew as we stood there, not caring that our comrades witnessed our unusual display of affection, that we were more than friends. We were brothers, brothers as much as any men of one blood.

An instant later the moment was over and Holmes and I drew our weapons to check their readiness. The others observed our silent signal, and set to work preparing their own firearms for this second of crucial assaults.

"I believe we can go in now," Holmes told Atkins.

We moved quickly down the wide surface tube and made straight for the brightest source of light which we knew came from the high doorway of the rocket chamber. Once there, we entered and could see, in the unnatural light of the sun crystals, several guards laying unconscious around the wheeled platform that held the second of Ling's great dragons. From the look of things, they had apparently attempted to make a launch before succumbing to the gas. Two of the four chains which secured the rocket to its mobile base had been unfastened. And the platform had been moved to within ten feet of the shaft's tall doorway on the metal guide tracks.

"Dear Lord!" Atkins whispered in horror. "They were really going to do it." He then gritted his teeth and called to the men. "Set the charges and wait for my signal before you start the timers."

It was at that moment I realized that Holmes was not with us. He had continued on alone into a deeper portion of the caverns, and I knew well what he was about. Mephistopheles was down there somewhere, and my associate had gone to find him. I, too, was anxious to move on. For I knew that if he were down there, Emily's son would most likely be also.

"Inspector!" I shouted. "Holmes has gone on ahead. He may need our help!"

"Yes," Charlie answered. "You men secure these prisoners. Field Marshal, you'd best come with Watson and me."

We left the unconscious men to the rest of our team, and made our way down several long tunnels, each descending deeper into the subterranean fortress. I began to feel as though we were lost, when suddenly we heard a call.

"Watson! Over here!"

It was Holmes.

We ran in the direction of his cry and found an open door that led into a small room. Upon entering, we found my colleague standing all alone with what looked like a piece of cloth in his hand. The only furniture to be found was a small bed, a desk, and a chair. The room was dimly lit by an oil lamp that hung on the far wall, and there was an ashtray on the desk with a long cigar that sat on the lip and was still smoldering.

"What have you found, Holmes?" I asked.

"A child's shirt," he answered, handing it to me. "He was here with the boy, Watson, only moments ago."

"But where is he now?" I puzzled.

"I'm not sure, my friend," he replied, looking about. "He couldn't have gotten past me. I came the only way in or out."

Suddenly having spied something near the wall, Holmes leapt forward and pushed aside the small bed. There, behind the headboard, was an opening, a narrow shaft that appeared to angle upward.

"Quickly!" my associate shouted. "He's headed for the surface. Charlie, where did you place the men outside?"

But the inspector did not answer.

150

"Charlie," Holmes repeated, "where are your men?"

But he continued to stand silent, almost as though he were in shock.

Finally Atkins stepped over to him and took hold of his right arm in an effort to break the inspector's strange trance.

"I say, Charlie, did you get a breath of that gas?"

"There are no men," Charlie said slowly, still frozen in place.

"What did you say?" I asked, unsure of his meaning.

"There are no men at the surface. We're all down here."

"Charlie," Holmes spoke in disbelief, "why?"

"It seemed so unnecessary." The inspector turned away. "It seemed so unnecessary."

It was then that I realized that the worst had come to pass. Charlie had made the fatal error, and we had not stopped him.

Just then, Lee Ho appeared in the doorway.

"We have discovered the main vault, gentlemen, but neither the book of war nor the location of the third dragon were to be found."

"Field Marshal," Holmes said with quiet resolve, "I need a man to get a message to the nearest telegraph office as swiftly as possible."

"Yes," he stammered, "yes, of course, Holmes."

My associate then seated himself at the desk and scratched a hurried note. I remember it painfully well, for I held the lamp at his side as he penned the desperate words. It read:

My Dear Queen,
With all my heart--with all my being--with all my soul I beg you--flee London.

Sherlock Holmes

Chapter Six

And I saw, as it were, the third dragon setting high upon a mountain top. And I marveled at its beauty as it stood in awesome majesty; its red skin gleaming in the early morning sunlight--the image of the terrible winged beast glaring at me as though it were truly alive. There was no wind at all, not even the slightest breeze. Nor was there any sound from animal or insect. I could hear nothing but my own breath which was ever so soft and shallow, with only the steady beat of my heart for company.

Suddenly, without warning or reason, the great rocket lifted skyward, but there was no smoke or flame that could be seen. It seemed to be powered by some evil magic, and it made no noise at all.

And, as though I had wings, I too, leapt into the sky and traveled along with the dragon at its side, noticing at once that we were a great distance above the English countryside. I began to recognize the landmarks below and could even see my boyhood home, although it seemed I should have been miles away from that part of England.

It was then that the highest peaks of the buildings of some distant city became visible to me. And we, the dragon and I, began to descend as though it had mystically been determined that this was where we were to go.

Ever so slowly the outlines of the structures took form. And as we drew closer, there could be heard the faintest tones of distant church bells.

<u>Yes</u>, I thought, <u>I know this place. But why can I not make it out</u>?

We were almost directly over the city when it struck me like a bolt of lighting. <u>This is London</u>.

I now knew well where we were, and why we had come--the dragon to destroy, and I to observe.

I looked down to behold the city just waking up, and I could see the streets and the market places beginning to fill with people; people by the thousands, going about their daily business quite unaware of our presence above. The merchants were making their deliveries, and I could hear the cabbies calling their good mornings to one another. And then I saw the children in the school yards; all the tender children of London playing carelessly in the early morning sun.

Suddenly the great dragon stopped, stopped in midair, and roared a mighty and terrible roar. This caused all below to cease from their work and their play, and look up in horror at the fearsome beast which stood poised and ready to strike. And at that moment, every man, woman and child realized what was to happen. And I looked upon their frightened faces and called to them.

<u>Forgive me! I did all that I could! Forgive me!</u>

Then, without warning, the dragon moved again and plummeted towards the heart of the city with another terrible roar. But the people did not run, for they knew that there was no place to hide. And as the dragon was upon them, they suddenly cried out, as if with one voice, and I shouted with them.

"Noooooooo! . . ."

"Watson, wake up! Watson, wake up, you're dreaming."

It was Holmes.

I had, indeed, been dreaming, and was now sitting up in my bed, drenched in a cold sweat, staring wide-eyed at my companion.

"It's all right, Watson," he reassured me, "just take a few deep breaths and sit a bit."

I was still quite shaken from the nightmare, and I spoke to my associate in a quivering voice.

"My God, Holmes, the humanity."

Just then Mrs. Hudson appeared in the doorway with a few of the other tenants who had also heard my cry.

"Is the doctor all right?" she asked with concern.

"Yes," Holmes answered, "it was just a nightmare. He'll be fine."

"Perhaps a spot of tea would help. It would be no trouble to make you some, Doctor Watson."

"No, thank you, Mrs. Hudson," I said, starting to collect myself. "I'm sure I'll be all right, but thank you for offering."

"If you're sure then, Doctor?" she said kindly.

"Yes, thank you, I'm sure."

They then returned to their rooms, leaving Holmes and I alone once more.

"Oh, Holmes," I sighed, "you wouldn't believe the dream I just had."

"Yes, I would, Watson," he replied. "Considering the way things went last night, it's a wonder we can sleep at all."

It was now the evening after our raid on Ling's Aylesbury installation. We had returned to London that morning with the prisoners, and informed the government that an evacuation of the city should be prepared at once. It was decided that the military and the local law enforcement would organize the evacuation, and that Field Marshal Atkins would head the entire operation. The Queen who, after receiving Holmes's telegram, refused to leave the city until the evacuation had begun, gave Atkins twenty-four hours in which to formulate his plan and begin the exodus. Holmes and I had spent the entire day helping Atkins with the planning, and had returned home that evening exhausted, due to having gone more than thirty-six hours without sleep. It had been shortly after six o'clock that evening when we took to our beds, and it was now about ten-thirty. We had wanted to get as much rest as possible, for the evacuation was to begin at sunrise the following day. But my nightmare had gotten us up after about only four hours, and I felt sorry for waking my friend from the sleep he needed so badly.

"Why don't you go back to bed, Holmes? You've had less sleep than I the past few days. I think I'll step up on the roof and get a bit of fresh air."

"I'll go with you, Watson," he smiled, placing a friendly hand on my shoulder. "I could use a little night air myself."

We were both still fully clothed, as we had collapsed into our beds that evening, not even bothering to remove our shoes. Once on the roof, we looked out over the city and stood in silence for a while. It almost seemed as though we were saying a quiet farewell to an old friend, an old friend who was about to die.

"Oh, Holmes," I said, breaking the stillness, "how can this be happening?"

"I don't know, Watson," he answered. "But it is."

"What can Ling possibly gain from this senseless destruction?" I growled. "What victory can there be in the ashes? What glory in the blood of children?"

"Madness has no reason, Watson. It does not require compassion, only the means to an end."

It all seemed so impossible to me. And now, even though the end had come, I found it hard to believe.

"Did you speak with Charlie today, Holmes?"

"No, Watson. As soon as we reached the city this morning, he went straight to the Yard and attempted to resign his post. The prime minister made sure it was not accepted, of course. I had a feeling Charlie would do something like that, so I contacted Disraeli as soon as we returned, and we both agreed that the inspector was much too valuable a man to be lost, despite his error last night. As I understand, Charlie has been put in charge of security at the museum. He's also responsible for getting the most precious works of art out with the evacuation in the morning."

"Poor Charlie," I sighed. "I've never seen a man more broken than he was last night. And who's to say we could have prevented an escape even if there had been a few men left at the surface."

"Precisely, Watson," he agreed.

"Nevertheless, Holmes, what's done is done. Surely Ling knows of our actions by now. I'm quite frankly a bit surprised he hasn't finished it yet. What do you think he's waiting for?"

"Hard to say, my friend. Perhaps he thinks we may panic and still come through with the ransom. Or maybe he'll take one last shot at stealing the Ming artifacts that he's so obsessed with. I just don't know."

We said nothing more for a short while after that. But then another concern crept into my mind.

"I wish Emily had stayed in Aylesbury as I requested," I told my associate. "But she insisted she would return home in the event that some news of her son should come. What do you think, Holmes? Is there any chance the boy is still alive?"

"There's always a chance, Watson," my colleague said with encouragement. "The one thing we must never let go of is hope."

Hope indeed, thought I. But how could there be hope at such a time? Our assault on the Aylesbury fortress had allowed us to destroy the second terrible dragon, and capture Ling's telegraph codes as well. But since we were unable to find the location of the third rocket, or the book of war, not to mention having been unable to save Emily's poor son, the operation seemed worse than a complete failure. It was the death sentence for all of London. And now that all hope appeared out of our grasp, there seemed no reason for despair, only acceptance.

"Tell me, Holmes," I said, letting my heart go numb, "did you happen to look under your bed as Finny suggested, just to be sure the dragon's not really there, I mean?"

"No, Watson," he answered with a laugh, "I suppose I should take the time and--"

Suddenly he froze in place, not budging an inch nor blinking an eye, his mind a whirlwind of thought within.

"What is it, Holmes?" I asked curiously. "What have you found?"

An instant later he leapt forward and took me firmly by the shoulders, shouting at the top of his lungs.

"By heavens, Watson, you have done it!"

"Done what?" I said, quite confused.

"Don't you see, Watson? I know where the third dragon is. It's under my bed. It's under my nose. It's in the very spot Ling's been trying to tell us. Morlock Castle. What a fox he is. He knew that by making it so obvious to me, I would never take that possibility seriously. Of course it's at Morlock Castle. The very last place in all of England that I would look.

"Come, Watson, there's not a moment to lose. You signal Lee Ho and his sons with the lanterns, and I'll contact Charlie and Atkins so they can reassemble the assault team."

"Whatever you say, Holmes," I said, a bit bewildered.

I had a thousand questions to ask him at that moment, but there was no time for them. I set the signal lamps, as he had requested, and then returned to my room for a change of clothes. It was evident to me that we would be going to Dover that night, and I wanted to feel as fresh as possible.

Holmes had bolted down the stairs and left the building with great haste. So when I heard the front bell ring at this odd hour, I assumed that he was back to collect something he had forgotten, and was most probably without a key. Racing down the stairs, not wanting him to be delayed, I hurried to the door and opened it quickly.

But to my surprise, it was not Holmes on the step, but Maggy, Emily's servant and friend, who was standing before me with a most somber expression on her face.

"Why, Maggy," I said a bit awkwardly, "what brings you here?"

"Pardon me, Doctor," she said, her lower lip trembling, "but I must tell you . . . I must tell you . . ."

But she could not continue. Large tears rolled down her worn face and she began to sob deeply.

"Please come in quickly," I told her, taking her hand and leading her to the sitting-room sofa. "Now please, Maggy, try to calm yourself and tell me what's wrong. Is Emily all right?"

"No, sir, she's not," the poor woman began slowly. "She made me promise not to tell you, but I just can't keep it anymore."

"Not to tell me what, Maggy? Please, you must be open with me."

"Yes, sir, I know that now," she answered. "This morning, after you arrived back, Emily came home, but she did not stay for long."

"What do you mean?" I pressed.

"She's gone to Dover to see that awful Ling fellow. She's gone to be with her son at that dreadful castle. I tried to stop her, Doctor, but you know how hard-headed she can be."

"I do indeed, Maggy," was my reply. "Do this for me, will you? Go back to your house and wait there in the event that she should return home. As for Ling, leave that scoundrel to us. I've quite had my fill of that man, and I mean to finish it, once and for all, this very night."

I walked with her to the street then, and saw her to her cab. The moment she had left, I hurried back inside and made for the roof, as I wanted to be sure the signal lamps were bright and visible. It was not long before the dark silhouette of the strange airship came into view, just rounding the large tower which housed Big Ben.

I made ready for their landing by taking a lantern in each hand and standing directly over the spot they were to set down. Their arrival was graceful and precise, and I stepped back allowing room for the docking.

"We must go to Dover tonight," I said, rushing forward to greet them. "Do you have enough fuel to take us that far?"

"Yes, Doctor," Lee Ho answered, "more than enough. But I thought you did not enjoy traveling in our skycraft," he said with a subtle smile.

"I don't," I replied bluntly. "But tonight I would ride on the back of a dragon if I thought it would get me to Dover any faster."

An instant later, Holmes's head popped through the small door on the floor of the roof.

"Are we ready then?" he asked briskly.

"Yes, Holmes," I answered with conviction. "Let's go and send that devil back to hell where he belongs."

"Right you are, Watson," he replied with the same conviction while pulling himself up to join us. "The team is being reassembled now, and they will be leaving for Dover by train shortly. All the tracks are being cleared, and Charlie and Atkins are being relieved of their duties here so they can lead the team."

"Capital!" I exclaimed as we started to board the airship .

"I also made sure they were ready to deal with an attack on the museum," Holmes added. "If Ling is going to try one last time to steal the Ming treasures, I'm sure it will be tonight."

"Oh, Mr. Holmes," said Lee Ho, "I must tell you something."

"What is it, my friend?" he asked.

The old Oriental then whispered something to him which caused my associate to retrieve a small pad from his pocket and scratch a hurried note. He then jumped from his seat and ran to the small door on the floor of the roof. Poking his head through, he shouted at the height of his voice.

"Mrs. Hudson!"

No doubt he awakened, not only everyone in our building, but half of the rest of the street as well.

It was not long before she appeared, sleepy and startled, at the bottom of the ladder.

"What is it, Mr. Holmes?" she asked with surprise.

"Mrs. Hudson, you're a good patriot, aren't you?"

"I most certainly am," she answered standing straight and proud.

"And you know that we have been working with Scotland Yard on a very important case, don't you?"

"Well, yes, I have seen you with Inspector Whittington."

"Well then, it is imperative that you get this message to the head of security at the London Museum as quickly as possible. Do you understand?"

"No, I don't understand," she answered, "but I'll do as you say, Mr. Holmes. You can count on that."

"Thank you, Mrs. Hudson," he said with a wink. "I love you."

"Save it for the rent time," she told him as she blushed and ran off to her room to change.

"All right then," Holmes said with satisfaction, "let's be off."

And so we were; off to Morlock Castle to try and put an end to this nightmare. We were quick to catch the evening breeze, and Lee Ho held the throttle at full open as we sped through the night like some dark avenging angel determined to crush the evil that had oppressed us for so long. We were beyond the city in no time at all, and out over the countryside which was very distinguishable in the bright light of the full moon.

"Gentlemen," Lee Ho began, "I am going to take us to a very high elevation in order to prevent our being seen from the ground," he paused, "or the air."

"What do you mean, the air?" I asked.

"You will soon see, Watson," Holmes told me. "If our deduction is correct, we should pass over them somewhere along the way."

"Pass over who?" I puzzled.

But I did not have long to wait to find out. For Holmes had no more than spoken when Soong spied a dark shape passing several yards below us. It was Ling's own skyship descending towards the outskirts of the city, undoubtedly seeking a place to land and wait for a later hour of the night to strike.

"Do you think they've seen us?" I asked.

"I don't believe so," Lee Ho answered. "Since we were above them, their balloon should have obstructed their view."

"But shouldn't we return and warn those at the museum?"

"Not necessary, Watson," Holmes told me. "Mrs. Hudson is doing that for us at this very moment. You see, Lee Ho reminded me of just such a possibility before we left. Charlie's people will be ready for them tonight."

"Glad to hear it," I said gleefully. "But what about the possibility of Ling himself being on board?"

"Not a chance, Watson." Holmes's brow wrinkled. "He would never leave that last dragon after what we did to the other two. The rocket is his last defense, his last chance to regain the throne of China. He won't leave it until he has launched it, or until we have destroyed it."

"Let us hope that it is the latter of the two," said I. "I shudder to think what will happen if we fail this time."

And so we continued on.

But now I must break away from this point in my record and tell you of what took place later that night when eight of Ling's finest men made a last attempt to procure the precious Ming artifacts from the London Museum. I was not there, of course. But I have it on good account from Scotland Yard burglary specialist Samuel Van Ressen, who replaced Charlie as head of security that night, that what I am about to pen is accurate and complete.

It was about three that morning when Ling's men began to descend towards the roof of the museum from the west. They had apparently held off until this late hour in the hope of catching the security men off guard and drowsy. During their approach they passed over at still a fairly high altitude in order, we assume, to check the roof for soldiers and count their number. Having spotted only seven men on the east side, hence their approach from the west, they circled round and adjusted their height so as to complete the landing. We came to know later that each one of these men was highly skilled in the martial arts, and that they were quite deadly and very capable of taking on a security force several times their number. So it was no wonder that seven soldiers and the thought of four times as many within the museum did not deter them from their mission.

As they moved closer and closer to the roof, it must have seemed to them that their victory was assured. But while they were yet some twenty yards from their proposed landing point, Van Ressen called the attack. Twenty men crawled from under blankets that had been covered with gravel, and each one was an archer of great skill. Rushing forward with their bows in hand, they formed a hurried line near the edge while a few of them lit their fire arrows, passing the flame from tip to tip with their comrades.

Seeing what was about to take place, the navigator of the doomed skyship turned the vessel hard to port in an effort to attempt an escape. But this maneuver only served to bring the craft around broadside, which gave our marksmen an even bigger target to aim at. An instant later, Van Ressen called "fire," and twenty flaming arrows went streaking through the night; not towards the men in the ship, mind you, but directly at the large balloon which was their only hold on the sky. The first arrow had no more than touched the leathery side when the large, cigar-shaped bulb erupted into a massive ball of fire and dropped the disabled craft beneath it like a stone.

For, you see, Lee Ho had informed Holmes that the gas used in this airship was extremely flammable, almost explosive, making the craft's destruction an easy matter. Anyone who had ever read the book of war would know this, but apparently Ling had underestimated his formidable cousin.

In all, five of Ling's men died instantly in the fiery crash; another passed away later that morning due to severe burns. The other two would live to stand trial for their crime, although they would never speak of it to anyone. They would never speak of it because, upon close examination of the bodies, it was discovered that each man's tongue had been cut out. They had done this to themselves voluntarily in order to prove to their master, Ling, that their obedience to him was complete. It was their way of saying that their lot in life was to obey, not to question. These were the cream of Ling's best trained and most fanatic assassins, and could be identified by the image of a dragon which they had burned into their flesh on the side of their upper left arms. When I heard of it, I recalled how the two Orientals who had been killed by the crocodiles in the Paris sewer had not cried out at all. This was because they could not. For when their tongues were cut out, they also severed their vocal cords. Such was the demise of these men.

But before all of this took place, you will remember, we were speeding towards Morlock Castle bent on defeating the evil which possessed it.

As Lee Ho steered us toward the sea, the startling white cliffs of Dover suddenly became visible in the bright moonlight. We would follow the shoreline until we came close to our destination. Once near, it was agreed that we would set down behind the woods adjacent to the castle and make our way from there on foot.

I was ready for this confrontation. This villain, Ling, had taken the woman I loved and her son, not to mention my peace of mind. He had threatened the city that was my home, and the innocent people who lived there with me. Make no mistake, I meant to be done with this problem of a man.

It was well after two when the tall, dark battlements of Morlock Castle came into view, and their image seemed all the more sinister that night as a heavy shroud of mist enveloped the entire structure like some vile spirit come to perform some unholy ritual on this, the first night of the full moon. The castle appeared completely dark and deserted as we searched for some kind of activity in or around it. But no one was to be seen nor was there any sound that could be heard, only the chirping of the frogs in the pond and the crickets in the woods and brush. As we settled down slowly behind the trees, I could feel a cold shiver run down `my spine at the thought of Emily and her son being held hostage in so terrible a place. Holmes was also moved by the sight, but in a different way.

"Well," he began with a sigh, "you can rest assured that we are expected tonight."

"What makes you think that, Holmes?" I asked.

"You saw it, Watson. Reason it out for yourself. By now Ling knows there will be no ransom. He also knows that two of his rockets have been destroyed and that we would come for him even if we were unable to locate his third dragon, which we have."

"But are you sure," I questioned, "that the third rocket is really here? Perhaps he has left the castle with Emily and her son and gone to some other location where the rocket might be."

"Oh, no, Watson," he said with a hardened stare, "Ling is here all right. I can feel him. And where Ling is, the dragon is also. Mephistopheles is here as well; Emily, her son, and all of Ling's men. They're all here, Watson. And what happens here tonight will determine the future of the world, in a sense. For some strange reason it has come down to that."

He then turned and spoke softly to Lee Ho. "Tell me, sir, do you believe in God?"

"Why, yes," the old man answered. "Why do you ask?"

"Because one or more of us may die tonight, and I would like to think that one day I might share your company beyond this life."

"I am sure it will be so," the old man said with conviction, and then turned his attentions to bringing our craft in for a soft landing.

Once on the ground we were quick to secure the ship and make ready our weapons. After that, we crept through the woods in silence until the bleak towers of the castle came into

164

view. As I scanned the cold silhouette of the old structure, it still appeared as deserted as before, with no light or sound to indicate otherwise. But I perceived that Holmes was also studying the situation, and it seemed to me from the strange turn of his head that he was seeing the same image as I, only with different eyes. After a few moments like this, he turned to Lee Ho and his sons.

"I think it would be best if we split up, gentlemen. Watson and I can make our way up to that side window," he said, pointing, "and enter on the top floor. If you and your sons are able to find access on the ground floor, possibly from the rear of the castle, it would be very advantageous for us. If any of us are killed or captured, the others may still be able to find the rocket and disable it. Of course, we want to find Miss Cantaville, her son, and your book of war. But the rocket launch must be stopped whatever the cost."

"Yes, Mr. Holmes," the kindly old man nodded. "I agree with your reasoning." And with that, he and his sons slipped away into the shadows. They had already disappeared from our sight when a quiet voice returned one last reply: "Until we meet again, my friends."

After which the night gave way to the silence once more.

Holmes and I then started our own trek towards the castle, keeping ourselves low while creeping towards the north side where the window my associate had singled out was located. As we neared the sheer greystone wall, I whispered to my companion a grave concern of mine.

"Excuse me for asking, but how do you propose we reach that window without a rope?"

"Quite simple, Watson," he answered. "We climb."

"Climb what?" I asked, unsure as ever. "There's nothing to climb, not even a drainspout."

"This castle is very old, Watson. Much of the mortar is weatherworn, I'm sure. We'll have to feel our way up, of course, but there should be enough space between most of the blocks to allow us a fairly reasonable hold."

Standing at the base of the wall, I looked straight up at the window and felt myself become dizzy at the thought of such a climb. And I questioned my ability to perform such a difficult task.

"I don't know, Holmes," I said, a bit breathless. "I'm not sure that I can do it. You know my fear of heights."

"Yes, my friend, I do," he replied with understanding. "If you don't think you can make it, stay here and stand watch. Perhaps I will be able to find a way to let you in once I'm inside myself."

"But if I do that, Holmes," I said with regret, "you'll be alone. Who will guard your back?"

"Not to worry," he smiled, "I'll be all right."

"Yes, you will be," I remarked, taking control of my fears, "because I'm going with you. Now let's get started."

It seemed easy at first, for there were large gaps between the stones which permitted a firm grip and a relatively secure foothold on the old wall. In no time at all we were almost halfway up. But then the gaps turned spotty and it became more and more difficult to find a comfortable grasp. We were now several feet above the ground, and I could feel my fingertips starting to burn as I was forced to use less of a full grip to support myself. This slowed our pace considerably, causing us to hunt for each hold with painstaking care. Finally, when we were no more than six feet below the window, I could find no gap for support no matter where I tried. My fingertips were now on fire with pain, and every time I looked down my dizziness returned. In desperation I spoke out to Holmes who was to my right and slightly above me.

"Holmes . . . Holmes, I can't find a hold. I don't know if I can make it."

"Stay calm, Watson," was his reassuring reply. "I'll help you. I'm going to edge over a bit, and I want you to take hold of my leg."

"No, Holmes," I moaned in agony from the cramping in my hands. "If I do, I'll pull us both down. Go on without me."

"Not on your life, Watson. Now do as I say. I have a firm grip."

The pain and fatigue became too severe for me to argue, so I took a deep breath and reached out with my right hand, catching my associate by the cuff of his trouser. But in doing so I suddenly slipped, losing my foothold, and dangled helplessly underneath Holmes, who was now forced to support both our weights.

It was then that I sensed something almost supernatural about my colleague. For he had held fast to the wall, his eyes straight ahead, his face without expression, and then he spoke as though he were feeling nothing at all.

"Just hold on, Watson, we're almost there. I'll finish the climb."

He then proceeded upward, taking each block ever so slowly. He made no sound, and each time he lifted the leg onto which I held, it was a strong, steady pull. Finally he reached the window, and with one mighty yank, pulled himself up to the waist and leaned inside.

"Now, Watson," he said in an even tone, "do you think you can climb up my leg and reach the sill?"

"Yes, Holmes," I answered, "I think I can."

Pulling myself up, I found a grip just below the window, and in a matter of a few short moments bypassed my friend and entered the castle. Taking hold of his wrists, I brought him inside, where he fell to the floor, utterly exhausted. It was then that I noticed that blood was running from every one of his fingertips, and that he was staring blankly at the ceiling, almost as though he were in shock.

"Oh, Holmes," I said with great remorse. "I had no idea."

I bent down to check his pulse, which seemed remarkably slow and steady. And then, in an instant he looked at me and smiled like a man who had just finished a pleasant nap.

"Well, I see we're here," he said very matter-of-factly. "Help me to my feet and we can begin our search."

Needless to say, I was astounded. "But Holmes," I insisted, "your hands."

"My hands?" he replied, a bit bewildered. "Oh my, I see what you mean, Watson. Well, never mind them now. There are more important matters to attend to."

Extending my hand, I pulled him up and studied him carefully to see if he would, indeed, remain that way.

167

"Don't look so surprised, my friend," he told me. "You know I've been practicing the fine art of contemplation for many years. Remember, Watson, one should control his mind, it should not control him."

What could I say? The man was beyond my comprehension.

I turned around and beheld the large throne room in which, one month earlier, Mr. Ling had first made known to us his ransom demands and dreadful intentions for our great city of London. The room looked much the same as before, although it appeared that the large round table on which the charred remains of the miniature city were located had been removed. The heavy ornate throne still sat upon its pedestal directly in front of the massive curtain which bore the symbols of the three dragons, and the familiar gong which we now recognized from the other two installations was in its original spot next to the large chair. Surely this had to be the nest of the third dragon.

We had entered the room right next to the stairway which we had used on our first raid of the castle. So I stepped softly over to a window that was situated towards the front of the building, and briefly surveyed the outdoors to see if anyone was about. But there were no signs of life. I saw only the dark woods and the reflection of the full moon on the quiet pond below. And I thought about how much safer it would have been to make the climb we had just finished in front over the water, rather than the side wall with nothing underneath but the rocks to break our fall. But that would have increased the risk of our being seen beyond a reasonable level.

"Come, Watson," Holmes whispered as he started across the room, "let us see if I am indeed correct."

I caught up with him quickly and we moved silently towards the large curtain--our pistols in hand--scanning the room for anything out of the ordinary. An instant later we heard a short hissing sound, and I must have jumped three feet into the air as a loud firework exploded behind us. Whirling around, I saw nothing but a small puff of smoke near the place where it had landed, while there was still no indication of a human presence. Not knowing what to make of it, I turned once more towards the large throne, but this time it was not empty. For there, seated in the ornate chair, like some dark relic from the ancient Chinese monarchy, was the infamous Chang Ling, dressed in the royal clothing of the Ming emperors of old. He held in his hand a long mallet, which I came to recognize at once as identical to those which I had seen at the Southend-on-Sea and Aylesbury installations: the hammer used to sound the gong that would fire the rocket.

He just stared at us without word or expression, and his eyes looked very much like those of the dragons painted on the curtain behind him.

We all stood motionless for what seemed the longest time; the tension was so great that even the air around us seemed too thick to breathe. Finally Ling tilted his head up ever so slightly, and broke the silence with a cold, firm voice.

"I must suppose that you gentlemen are here to deliver the ten million pounds and the Ming artifacts I requested."

But this, of course, was not the case, and Ling knew it well. For he had come to realize that the Crown would not bow to any man; not even the dragonmaster of the Orient. And he knew that to hope for this any longer was futile.

"Mr. Ming," Holmes now spoke in reply, "I implore you in the name of all that is honorable and good, in the very name of God, please turn from this most dreadful act and surrender yourself in a noble fashion, as is worthy of the honored and respected name of Ming. For I understand that you have been persuaded by the Englishman I call Mephistopheles to undertake this gruesome task, and I realize that his promises are sweet-smelling. But do not be fooled by the cup of gall that he extends to the world, and even to you. No good can come from violence and death. For violence and death only beget themselves. Remember that you are Ming, and remember what it means to be so."

I watched him closely then to see if my associate's plea had had some effect on the stone-faced man. But he remained without expression as he answered Holmes in the same cold tone as before.

"A marvelous performance, Mr. Holmes, I really did enjoy it. But I must assume you are telling me that you have not brought the ransom with you. Is that correct?"

My colleague sighed as he digested Ling's reply.

"You know that we have not," he told him. "We have come to destroy the third rocket and put an end to this madness."

"Well, then," Ling's voice rose now for the first time, "if that is why you are here, let me introduce you to the beast."

Clapping his hands sharply, he sat motionless as the huge curtain behind him was drawn to the side. And there, seated upon its platform, its chains unfastened and ready for launch, was the third and last dragon. But an even greater surprise was the sight of Emily tied in a chair seated right next to the rocket, with a young boy clutching her hand who, while not restrained, would not leave his mother's side.

Ling spoke again.

"You will now relinquish your weapons, gentlemen."

His men came quickly from out of the shadows and took our pistols, while one soldier moved over to Emily and began untieing her. As the guards bound our hands behind us, Emily was brought to our side with young Jeffry still holding her arm tightly.

He was a handsome young boy with his mother's dark hair and steel blue eyes. And while one might have expected the poor lad to be in tears, he only glared at the guard who had escorted his mother, and sought to comfort her with soft, consoling words.

"It's all right, Mummy."

Holmes smiled at him when he heard his courageous reaction, and I, too, was impressed by the little fellow's strength in the face of such adversity.

"That's a good lad," my associate told him as we were led away towards the stairway.

"Mr. Holmes," Chang Ling spoke, causing the guards to stop us for a moment. "The dragon will be launched at sunrise. It is regrettable that so many will have to perish, but once I have taken the throne in China, I will see to it that financial restitution is made to your country."

"Oh, really?" Holmes said in quiet reply. "Just what is the price of murder?"

Ling made no answer. He only motioned with his hand which caused the guards to start us on our way once more.

Emily had been silent up to this point, but now she looked at me with a steady expression.

"I'm not sorry that I came here, John. I'm sure you don't approve. But Jeffry is my son, and that made the decision my own."

"I understand, Emily," I told her with compassion. "You are the most remarkable woman I have ever known."

"And one thing more, John," she said without pause, her eyes meeting mine. "I love you."

At the sound of these words, my spirit soared like a bird despite our grave situation, and I spoke my reply with heartfelt emotion.

"And I you, my dear. On that you may rest assured."

We were led down the stairway from the second floor to another set of stairs which brought us deeper into the lower sub-chambers of the castle. As we turned down a narrow hallway, I could see, in the flickering light of the torches, the doorways of several cells with iron doors, one of which, I was sure was about to become our prison. We presently approached a door to our right and paused, as there was a guard already there who appeared to be having some problem with the lock. He was turned away from us and was rattling the keys loudly while he mumbled to himself in Chinese. One of the four men who had led us to this place stepped forward to see what the difficulty might be, when suddenly the odd fellow spun around and kicked the guard square in the forehead.

"God save the Queen!" was his triumphant shout.

It was the young Chinaman, Wu.

An instant later, his brother Soong and Lee Ho leapt from an open cell behind us and engaged the guards one on one, lashing out with ferocious vigor as they were upon the surprised men in a matter of moments. The fighting was fierce and, for a short time, we were unable to determine who the victors might be. But eventually Lee Ho and his sons won out, although Wu did need a little assistance from his father in the end. One of the guards had pinned the young man to the floor and was about to strike at him with a clenched fist, when Lee Ho caught his hand in the air and put a well-placed knee to the side of his head.

Needless to say, we were elated to see our friends again, and we laughed and greeted each other warmly as they quickly removed our bonds. Once we were free, it seemed expedient to finish our work as soon as possible. But that meant returning to the second floor of the castle, and that would be a dangerous trek for anyone, much less a woman and a boy.

My associate looked at me with a determined gaze, and placed a friend's firm hand on my shoulder.

"I want you to take Miss Cantaville and the boy and find your way out. We'll take care of Ling and his dragon."

"Yes," Lee Ho agreed, "it is best, Dr. Watson. We cannot expose them to any further danger."

"All right," I said with true sorrow. "I'll try to get them out safely. Please be careful, my friends."

Lee Ho then turned and pointed down the way.

"If you follow this passageway down to the end, you will find a ladder which leads up to a small study located to the rear of the castle. That is where we entered, through the window nearest the south wall. It will appear to be closed, but we left it ajar. It's your best chance."

"Thank you, once more, for everything," I told him. "I pray we will meet again."

"Dr. Watson," he added, "will you do me one favor?"

"What is that?" I asked.

Going back into the cell from which he had surprised our captors, he presently returned carrying an odd-looking box that appeared to be about two feet wide by one foot high, but only a few inches in depth. The Chinese symbols on its side were embroidered in bright gold and there were straps on either side so that it could be carried on one's back like a field pack. From the top I could see there protruded the tip ends of several scrolls which, from their apparent discoloration, appeared to bear the look of great age.

"This, Dr. Watson," Lee Ho spoke again, "is the book of war. We found it in the study. I and my family would be honored if you would receive it into your care. In the event that neither I nor either of my sons survive this night, I ask that you might retain it safely until such time as another member of our family should come to England in search of it. This, of course, is entirely your decision. No offense will be taken if you refuse."

I looked deep into the old man's weathered eyes and perceived his peace within. And, although they were well-worn with age, there was no doubt at all that these were the eyes of an honorable man. Reaching out, I took hold of one strap.

"I should be quite honored to do so," I said softly. "And you may rest assured that I will guard it with my very life."

"Thank you, sir," he replied, and then released the precious heirloom from his grasp.

"You'd best be going, Watson," Holmes said as I slung the article on my back. "Get Miss Cantaville and the boy out."

"All right then," I conceded.

With that we were off down the narrow hallway, but I suddenly felt compelled to take one last look at my companion, who was now helping Lee Ho and his sons secure Ling's guards in one of the empty cells. His eyes then met mine.

"If I don't make it," he called back ever so quietly, "I'll meet you on the other side."

I nodded my acknowledgement as they set off towards the stairs and disappeared from view. I remember that I wanted to linger a bit more, but was quick to push the feeling away and continue the short trek down the narrow passage, looking in all directions for the ladder of which Lee Ho had spoken.

When we finally reached the end of the hall, I spied it in the corner to my left, and could see that it indeed led straight up to a small trap door on the ceiling.

"You and Jeffry had better remain here until I can determine if it's safe," I told Emily.

"All right, John," she answered with concern, "but please be careful."

"I will," I replied reassuringly, and then made my way up the narrow passage.

173

When I reached the top, I slowly pushed open the access and scanned the dark room for some sign of life. There appeared to be no one about, so I pulled myself up onto the floor of the study and stood to take one more look around. Satisfied that I was alone, I beckoned Emily to join me and extended my hand down to help her and Jeffry through the small opening.

An instant later, I spotted something atop a large desk located near one of the windows not far from where we stood. I would probably have missed it altogether had it not been for the bright moonlight that night. But my eye caught the slightest hint of a silver gleam which I came to recognize almost immediately. It was the gleam that I had admired countless times before. On long, lazy evenings I would sit for hours, while chatting with Holmes, and polish its nickel-plated surface until it shined like fine sterling. It was Mildred.

I rushed over to the desk and took hold of the familiar old pistol. It slid neatly into my hand, almost as though it were a missing puzzle piece finally restored to its proper place. And there, among a small pile of other handguns, was Holmes's old steady; I quickly recognized the well-worn hub of its milky pearl handle.

"This is just what the doctor ordered," I said to Emily as I tucked them both securely in my coat. "Now we'd best be off."

We moved on then to the window that Lee Ho had told us would be open. And sure enough, although it appeared latched, the window had indeed been forced, and was being held closed by a small chip of wood that was wedged between the wall and the window frame. Pulling the wedge free, I eased the window open slowly and glanced about to see if the way was clear.

We were at the rear of the castle, and I could see the quiet channel before us like a great sheet of fine crystal shining in the brilliant moonlight. It was then that I heard the sound of voices in the distance, and presently spied a ship anchored just off the shore, very near the large clump of rocks that Ling had used to demonstrate to Holmes and I, a month earlier, the lethal accuracy of his deadly dragons. It appeared it was being made ready for a journey, for I could see several smaller boats moving what looked like supplies and equipment in a steady stream from shore to ship.

"It looks like Ling has planned to make his escape by sea," I whispered to Emily.

Taking care to stay low, I lifted Jeffry to the ground and then his mother. We made our way around, first to the side of the castle that Holmes and I had scaled earlier, and then to the front where we finally arrived at the edge of the woods. Removing the book of war from my back, I looked at Emily with tender eyes and handed it over to her.

"My dear," I said gingerly, "do you think you could make your way to Dover without me? I know it's a great deal to ask of you, but . . . well, Holmes, you see . . . he's the most brilliant man I've ever known, but he can be so careless sometimes. He never watches his back."

Suddenly she raised a hand to still me, and a smile formed on her most lovely face.

"John, you know that I am well able to care for my son and myself. I have done so for many years. Besides, it is your loyalty to Mr. Holmes that makes me love you all the more."

"Thank you, my dear," I said, overcome with emotion, and then kissed her deeply as the small boy watched with a sarcastic smirk.

"Now go, John," she said as a single tear trickled down her soft cheek. "Tell Lee Ho I'll take good care of his book."

I then bent down on one knee and smiled at the boy.

"Keep your mother safe, lad," I told him, "and do whatever she tells you."

"I will, sir," he replied briskly and then gave me a little smile of his own.

"Don't worry, Emily," I said to comfort her. "I'll meet you in Dover tomorrow."

With that I left them, and could not help but wonder if I would indeed ever see my beautiful Emily again. But this was only for a moment, for now I knew that it would take all my mental energy to determine some way of getting back into the castle without being seen. Going back the way we had come would probably be easiest, I thought, but the study was too far away from the stairway that led to the second floor. If I entered there, I would have to pass through much of the main part of the first floor, and that would surely increase the likelihood of my being discovered.

Finally I decided to attempt entry through the kitchen window that Holmes and I had used on our first raid of the castle. It seemed a reasonable risk, for I knew it was very near the stairway, and also I was sure that, from the number of men I had seen loading the ship, most of Ling's guards were occupied with that endeavor and would not be patrolling the hallways.

I forced the window as quietly as I could and made my way inside the dark space. Then, feeling my way to the door, I opened it ever so slightly and squinted through the crack. The hall appeared to be deserted and I heard nothing. So, with careful steps, I entered the passageway and crept towards the stairway with Mildred in my hand, her trigger cocked and ready.

Once there, I bolted up the stairs on the tips of my toes, and stopped just before the top in order to check the area for guards. Peeking over the stone railing, I could see no one at all which was a bit disappointing. I had hoped that Holmes, Lee Ho and his sons would have made it here by now.

I proceeded into the large room and moved quickly towards the great rocket which was still setting ready for launch, ever silent, ever awesome. But this time I noticed the large open trap door in the ceiling above it, and could clearly see the large full moon from where I stood.

An instant later, someone grabbed me from behind and placed a cupped hand across my mouth. I struggled to release myself when suddenly my attacker spoke.

"What are you doing here, Watson?"

It was Holmes.

"Is that Mildred I see in your hand?"

"Yes, it is," I said, breathing a sigh of relief, "and I brought a present for you."

As I pulled his old steady from my coat, Lee Ho and his sons stepped from the shadows and joined us.

"Good to see you again, Dr. Watson," Lee Ho remarked. "You certainly made the trip to Dover and back with remarkable speed."

"Yes . . . well . . . you see . . ." I began, a bit embarrassed, "Emily and her son are quite all right, and your book is safe and well."

"You need not say anything more," the old man chuckled, "I quite understand."

"Where did you find our revolvers?" Holmes asked as he checked the chamber and placed his in his coat.

"In the study, old boy, setting right out in the open."

"Then our luck is holding," Holmes remarked while giving me a friendly pat on my back. "And it's ever so good to see you again, Watson. You don't know how lucky I consider myself to have you for a companion."

There was much I wanted to say to him at the moment; much that needed to be said. But I knew that there was no time for such matters, so all I was able to muster was a quiet, "Thank you, Holmes."

Lee Ho turned his head for an instant, allowing us to enjoy the moment, but presently he, too, felt the need for haste and reluctantly broke the short silence.

"We must finish our work, gentlemen. Chang's hour is soon upon us."

"Yes, of course," I agreed, "let's be at it. What have you decided to do with the rocket?"

"We're going to launch it, Watson," Holmes said plainly.

"You're going to do what!" I exclaimed in astonishment. "You can't be serious."

"It's all right, Watson," my associate assured me. "We're going to reattach one of the support chains that is used to stabilize the rocket on its platform. We will then fasten the other end of the chain to an object of the weight needed to pull the firework in the direction of the sea. And, I believe," he said, pointing with one finger, "that that is the spot where the chain should be secured."

Looking up, I spied the small metal loop he had indicated, near the tip of the rocket on the side that did indeed face the channel. An instant later, Soong grabbed one of the chains from the floor and started shinnying his way up the sleek dragon.

"Oh, Holmes," I said with grave reservations, "it seems so very risky. If the weight is not heavy enough it could cross the channel and land somewhere in France. On the other hand, if the weight is too great, it could land a few yards away and --"

"--and kill us all," my associate finished the sentence. "You're quite right, Watson. And it really wouldn't do for us to lend our problems to the French. So I suggest that we choose an object which we deem slightly too heavy and take our chances with the rocket falling short."

Having fastened the chain tightly to the loop, the agile young man slid quickly down to the platform and leapt to the floor. It would have been a simple matter to attach the chain to the platform itself, but we all agreed that it was much too large for the modest opening above our heads. That being the case, we all spread out and started searching the room for some object that might be suitable to our purpose. A minute or two later we regrouped again, each one of us with an object for consideration.

Holmes had found an old battle shield that had been part of a decorative wall arrangement, while Lee Ho held in his hand an odd-looking porcelain vase that appeared to have a convenient handle for securing the chain. Soong and Wu had helped each other carry over a small metal table, but we quickly decided that it would be much too heavy for our purpose. Finally, I had come upon a two-foot-tall marble statue of an obscure Greek goddess who, I had to admit, was quite lovely, but also quite naked. This, of course, amused my associate and he could not resist commenting on my find.

"Oh, Watson," he taunted with a wry smile, "how unchivalrous of you."

"Very funny, Holmes," I replied sarcastically. "You should really be on the stage."

"Let me hold it," he said, extending his hands, and still chuckling to himself. "You may well have found just the thing, I think. What would you say it weighs, Watson, about three stone?"

"That would be my guess," I agreed.

Holmes then handed the young woman to Lee Ho for his opinion.

"Yes, it would seem about right," the kindly old man answered, "but I am not really familiar with this type of rocket. It is very hard to say if the weight is correct or not."

We all stood silent for a moment, but then Holmes spoke again.

"Well, I'm afraid we'll just have to take our chances with your newfound friend, Watson. There's no time for indecision."

We all agreed that the statue seemed to be about the right size and weight needed to pull the rocket in the direction of the channel--that is, as far as we could determine. Lee Ho instructed his son Wu to fasten it to the chain, and in a few moments we were ready for launch.

Holmes stepped over to the large throne beside which sat the long box that contained the gong's mallet. He stooped down and opened the case, taking a firm grip on its slender jaded handle.

"I'll sound the gong, gentlemen. I suggest you go to the other side of the room and prepare to move down the stairs quickly."

"Just one moment, Holmes," I protested. "I believe I should be the one to do it. If anything should go wrong, your remarkable talents are indispensable to the Crown. I, on the other hand, am only one of many common physicians in London and am, therefore, expendable."

"Gentlemen, please," Lee Ho interrupted, "there is no time for this. Besides, it is only logical that Soong should sound the gong, as he is the fastest runner among us."

Holmes and I paused for a moment, but then had to concede that he was indeed right. The young man was surely the fastest one present, and that meant that he was truly the most logical choice for the task.

My associate handed the mallet over to him as the spry Oriental bowed politely and smiled a confident smile.

"All right then," Holmes said briskly, "the rest of us go to the stairs."

We turned and started off as Soong stepped towards the gong, but an instant later five of Ling's men appeared at the top of the stairs. One of them spotted us and called a warning. For these were not the silent, elite fighters of Ling's ranks, but the laborers and craftsmen of his band. Nevertheless, we had been discovered and there was no time to lose if we were going to complete the launch.

Holmes called the charge and we rushed towards the men with the intent of engaging them only briefly, just long enough for Soong to sound the gong. But as we fought, the deep tone of the large metal symbol was not to be heard. After knocking one small fellow to the floor, I glanced backward and was horrified to see that the young man was locked in mortal combat with two black-clad figures who I immediately recognized as members of Ling's elite guard. There was no way of knowing where they had come from, but it was obvious that the unfortunate Soong was in desperate need of assistance. Realizing his own predicament, Lee Ho's clever son maneuvered the fight over closer to our battle, allowing his brother Wu to join him in the struggle.

In the process, he had been forced to drop the mallet in order to free his hands. I could see it lying on the floor very near the gong, but was unable to go after it, as a small man had taken hold of my leg and had set his teeth into my ankle. I yelped in pain as I fought to shake him loose, but he held on like a bulldog and even growled like one. His manner made me more angry than anything else, so in a fit of fury I drew Mildred from my coat and pointed her straight at his head.

Looking up, the small fellow froze as he stared at me wide-eyed; his teeth still deep in my ankle.

I then cocked Mildred's trigger and snarled the words: "Let--go."

There was, of course, very little likelihood that the man understood English. But Mildred spoke a universal language which he most definitely perceived. As he slowly released his grip, I pulled free and hurried over to the mallet, snatching it up with one hand while moving into striking position beside the large circular gong. I then drew it back and prepared to hit it soundly. But my intentions were stilled by a voice which spoke to me from across the room.

"If you launch the dragon, Dr. Watson," the cold monotone voice said, "I will kill Mr. Holmes."

Turning my head sharply, I came to recognize the one who had spoken as the infamous Chang Ling, who was standing but six feet from my associate with a pistol aimed directly at his chest.

The struggle was over now, and my companions stood surrounded by Ling's sentries, helpless to continue the fight any longer.

"I repeat, Dr. Watson," the dark Oriental spoke again, this time with clenched teeth, "if you sound the gong, I will shoot Mr. Holmes."

But my associate showed no fear, and at that moment he cried out himself.

"Do it, Watson! Do it now!"

Having heard his commanding voice, I drew back once more and prepared to strike. But still I could not bring it forward as the thought of Holmes's death flashed before me.

"You must, Watson!" Holmes called again with great fervor. "Think of London. Think of the people."

And so I thought of them. But still I could not sound the death sentence for my colleague.

Lowering the hammer slowly, I looked to Holmes with deep regret. But instead of seeing the disappointment I was sure would be in his eyes, I saw only the steady face which I had come to know so well through the years smiling ever so subtly at me. For, although I had failed him, he understood me right down to my very core. And he knew, beyond all doubt, that there was no way that I could ever purposely cause his demise.

I then dropped the mallet to the floor and walked over to join them. When I reached Holmes's side, I whispered my apologies to him softly.

"Forgive me, Holmes. I just couldn't."

"And now, gentlemen," the angry Ling snapped, "you have interfered with my plans for the last time."

"Cousin," Lee Ho now spoke, "why is it that you do not wear the emblem? Have you forgotten the ancient oath?"

With that, our friend reached into his shirt and retrieved a large gold medallion that was fastened to a thin chain around his neck. It was engraved with Chinese symbols, and he held it up so Ling could see it plainly. He then translated the words.

"The royal family of Ming. For truth and honor."

"I have my emblem, cousin," Ling answered sharply, "and I shall wear it again when I sit upon the throne of China, as is the destiny of Ming."

"And at what price will you do this?" Lee Ho asked. "At the expense of truth and honor?"

"You have grown weak in your old age," Ling replied. "Do you not see what those fools have done to our great land? I was among them when I studied for diplomatic service. I have seen their folly. But I convinced them to make me the acting ambassador. And now I will build my army, and my arsenal of great dragons. And I shall conquer them with great carnage so that truth and honor may reign once more under the emblem of Ming."

Chang was now quite agitated and he looked at my associate with fiery eyes.

"You, Mr. Holmes, have been the major cause for my losing the ransom. But no matter. The world shall know my might and fear me when they see the complete destruction of your London.

"I had intended to wait until dawn to launch the dragon. But now you shall witness the end before you die."

Holmes now came alive.

"What kind of creature are you, sir--you and that other devil. Those innocent people are still in their beds."

"It is regrettable that so many need die," Ling said with cold resolve. "And as for the Englishman, he was only a means to an end. But I am not completely without mercy, Mr. Holmes. If it is too painful for you to witness this deed, I will grant you a swift and honorable death."

This spoken, Ling aimed his pistol at my colleague and made ready to fire. An instant later, Lee Ho leapt in front of Holmes, taking the bullet square in the chest as Chang squeezed off the round. Our old friend then slumped to the floor while the surprised Chang watched with a stunned expression.

"God save the Queen!" Wu shouted, leaping forward with great ferocity and knocking the gun from his hand.

The struggle was on again as we all tangled once more, our fight renewed with vigor for the sake of our fallen comrade.

Holmes was quick to pounce upon Ling. And I dare say, considering his passionate state, he may well have killed him had not one of Ling's soldiers pulled him away in short order.

Hurrying to his feet, Chang raced over to the rocket and fought furiously to untie the marble statue from the chain. None of us were able to reach him, as we were all engaged in combat.

But then a miracle happened. The limp body of Lee Ho suddenly came to life as he sprang to his feet and dashed over to his cousin. They struggled beside the dragon; Ming against Ming, brother against brother, the fate of all of London in their hands.

It was then that I heard what sounded like distant thunder. But presently I came to recognize the noise as the rumble of approaching horses--several horses.

Being near one of the front windows, I managed to maneuver the man with whom I was fighting over to it and popped him sharply in the nose, setting him off balance for an instant. I then reached down and grabbed his ankles, pulling up quickly, and dumped him unceremoniously over the sill, sending him downward to an awkward splash in the pond below.

Looking into the distance, I suddenly caught sight of the horses I had heard. It was the assault group. They had finally arrived, and Emily and Jeffry were with them.

"It's Charlie and the others!" I called to Holmes.

But at that moment, Ling gave Lee Ho a mighty kick and sent our poor friend flying to a hard thump on the floor. I rushed over to help him, for I feared the fall had been too much for a man so badly wounded.

Most of Ling's men had fled by now, having caught sight of the assault team themselves. Only a few of the elite guards remained, and Lee Ho's sons kept at them.

I had just reached our friend's side when I observed that Ling had finally succeeded in untieing the statue from the chain. But he had no more than dropped it to the floor when Holmes was upon him once more; this time taking him from behind with great advantage.

It looked very much as though the victory would be ours, but a moment later young Wu landed a devastating blow to one of the guards and sent him hurling against the gong.

As his head bounced off the large metal sphere, the room resounded with the fullness of its deep tone. An instant later the rocket ignited, and smoke and fire began to spew from its bottom. Ling then turned within my associate's grasp, and they became locked in a death hold on one another.

"Watson, get out!" Holmes shouted as the fire and smoke increased. "Get out, all of you!"

By then I had lost sight of him in the fog. So, pulling Lee Ho to his feet, I made for a window and we all jumped for the safety of the pond; Lee Ho and I, his sons, and even Ling's elite guards.

Soong and Wu helped me pull their father to the shore as I watched the windows anxiously for some hint of my companion. But all that could be seen or heard was the dark smoke spewing from every opening of the second floor, and the deep roar of the dragon within.

"Holmes!" I cried, "My God, where are you!"

It seemed like an eternity, but suddenly, like a shot from a cannon, he burst from one of the windows, his coat on fire, and landed with a prodigious splash about thirty feet from where we were.

It was then that the terrible dragon appeared above the castle. With a mighty roar and a great display of fire and smoke, it moved upward slowly, lighting up the surrounding area in all directions with its brilliant tail flame.

I started to swim towards my companion, fearing that he had been seriously burned, but when he caught sight of me, he called out.

"I'm all right, Watson, but I fear the city is doomed."

And so he swam over to join us as the awesome dragon climbed ever higher into the heavens.

The assault team had reached us now, and gave chase to the remainder of Ling's people, most of whom were fleeing into the nearby woods.

We continued to watch the large firework as it pressed ever upward, and could finally observe its ever-increasing velocity. I knew that, although it was nearly dawn, the evacuation in London had not yet begun and that within a few minutes the dragon would most likely descend upon the very heart of the most densely populated part of our beloved city. It did, indeed, seem as though all was lost.

But then we were startled by the movements of this manmade dragon. For, instead of tilting inland as we were prepared to observe, it began to list seaward at an ever so slightly increasing angle. It was then that I first noticed the object dangling from the chain that we had attached to the rocket's tip, and I turned to my associate with great elation.

"You did it, Holmes! How did you get the statue refastened?"

"But, Watson, I didn't!" he said in amazement. "I broke free from Ling and then the fire forced me away."

"Then what is that?" I asked, quite confused.

Now Lee Ho straightened his head and gazed intently and knowingly at the strange object.

"That is not a statue," he said slowly. "I believe it is Chang Ling."

"Chang Ling!" I echoed in surprise.

And sure enough, in the struggle that had occurred between him and Holmes, Ling had somehow become entangled in the chain, and it was his charred, lifeless body that was pulling the third dragon out over the channel. Apparently we had greatly misjudged the weight necessary to divert the powerful rocket from its intended course, but now the ballast which was necessary to save our city was being provided by Chang himself.

Suddenly the rocket began to move downward.

"It should be far enough away," Holmes called to Charlie and Atkins who were on horseback nearby. "Let's go see what becomes of it."

Pulling ourselves from the water we ran around to the rear of the castle along the seashore. I had attempted to help Lee Ho with a supporting arm but I was amazed as he broke free of my grasp and ran ahead of me.

When we arrived at the edge of the white cliff, Emily and her son came to my side. We all stood in a long line, in great anticipation, as we observed the fiery mark--which was all we could see in the darkness--plummet ever closer to the earth.

"Cover your eyes!" Holmes shouted only moments before the rocket's impact.

And so we did. And I reached down and pulled Jeffry's head into my coat to shield him from the flash.

Suddenly all I could see was bright red. The brilliance of the light had penetrated my hand and eyelids. A few seconds later we heard a loud roar, like distant thunder, which grew in intensity and peaked with a mighty crescendo as the rocket exploded with fury. We could feel the heat from the great explosion, and I chanced to uncover my eyes in time to behold a massive fireball as it rose into the early morning sky. Ever upward it ascended in a great column of fire and ash, and climbed to a tremendous height where it umbrellaed out into an enormous, illuminated mushroom-shaped cloud.

We stood silent for a time, for there were no words at such a moment.

But then, out of the corner of my eye, I caught sight of a lone figure on horseback watching the spectacle from the edge of the woods.

"Look there," I told Holmes, who I suddenly noticed was already observing the solitary rider.

The shadow paused a moment more, and then disappeared into the trees. I then realized, as did my associate, that Mephistopheles had slipped through our fingers once more.

Holmes gave no indication of emotion. He turned back towards the sea.

"What is it the good book says, Watson? 'Surely the man who digs a trap for another will fall into his own pit.'"

"Yes, Holmes," I answered, "I suppose that's true enough."

With that, I turned and saw Emily handing Lee Ho his family's precious book. "I believe this belongs to you," she told him kindly.

"Yes, thank you," he replied. "I am honored that you have kept it for us."

"Now look here," I asked our friend, "why aren't you dead?"

The old Chinaman then smiled and lowered his head.

"It would seem that my ancestors have made their decision as to what is truth and honor."

Having spoken, he lifted up his large gold medallion and there, lodged in the soft yellow metal, was the bullet that his cousin had fired.

"You see," he said, "I am not wounded, Doctor, only bruised."

At that moment Charlie, Atkins, and Holmes came over to us.

"We're sending word to London to cancel the evacuation," Charlie told me.

"Yes," Atkins added, "our men are patching into the telegraph lines right now. We should be able to stop it before it even gets started."

"Wonderful," I concluded. "Then no one need ever know of the terrible catastrophe that almost happened."

"Yes, Watson," Holmes remarked with a satisfied grin. "I imagine it will be business as usual in London this morning."

And so we had finally put an end to the nightmare of Ling and his three dragons. And as the members of our assault team began bringing in the prisoners they had captured, we turned to take one last look at all that remained of Chang Ling's dream; a great, dark cloud which was just starting to drift with the early morning breeze.

With Emily and her son on my right, and Holmes to my left, I remember the feelings of warmth and completeness that I experienced at that moment. And then, as the first pink rays of the morning sun peeked over the horizon, the birds in the nearby woods began to sing, and so did my heart.

Chapter Seven

"Congratulations, Sir Johnathan Watson, and Sir Sherlock Holmes as well," Disraeli said merrily as he extended a warm hand for the shaking. "How does it feel to be knights of the realm, gentlemen?"

"Quite wonderful," I answered with delight, "the Queen was most gracious."

"Yes, it was a beautiful ceremony," the Prime Minister continued. "It's a pity that your knighthood must be kept secret, but you realize that if it were made public, people would want to know why you had received the honor, and since the entire matter is still top secret, that would be very hard to explain."

"We quite understand," Holmes told him, "don't we, Watson?"

"Yes, of course, Holmes," I answered half-heartedly. "It's all for the best."

Just then Charlie and Atkins entered the large sitting-room where we were. They, too, had been knighted by Her Majesty earlier that day, and the rest of the assault team, including Lee Ho and his sons, had received the Medal of Honor from the Queen.

The room we were in was the same one in which we had first met with Her majesty and Prime Minister Disraeli to notify them of Ling's demands almost a month ago. So, after greeting our comrades, my associate and I broke away for a moment and walked over to the large window that overlooked the beautiful, lamplit city beyond the palace.

It was a calm, clear evening, and I could see the reflection of the peaceful night in my friend's face.

"You know, Holmes," I began, "I always dreamed of being knighted by the Queen, and now that I have been, I can't tell a single soul."

"Yes, Watson," my associate laughed, "it is a bit ironic. But it's really not important, old friend. We know what we have done for Mother England, and in the end that's all that matters."

I then saw the slightest hint of a wrinkle in his brow, and I couldn't help but wonder what might possibly be bothering him on so triumphant an occasion.

"Is something wrong?" I asked softly.

And then he paused to take a deep breath.

"He's still out there, Watson--out there somewhere. And he has learned much from the book of war. One day we shall have to contend with him again." He then lowered his eyes and produced a broad smile. "But not tonight. Tonight the victory is ours."

At that moment I observed that Lee Ho and his sons had just arrived, and so I waved to them to join us. They were smartly dressed in fine silken Far Eastern garments, and it was plain to see that they were also of a royal lineage. When they reached us, each bowed deeply, while Holmes and I returned the greeting with a few small bows of our own.

I suddenly noticed that Lee Ho's clothes were dotted with the images of several small dragons, and I could not help but make a comment.

"I would have thought that you had had your fill of dragons by now."

"Oh," he said, realizing the reason for my statement, "yes, you see I was born in the year of the dragon. Oddly enough, so was my cousin Chang. Funny, I never thought of that before."

"Dear friend," Holmes said with great respect, "I know that we were all forced to move against Chang because of his threat, but even so, he was your relative. And, well . . . I just want you to know that you and your family have my deepest sympathies on his passing."

The old Chinaman paused for an instant, and I could see his eyes become misty.

"And mine as well," I told him. For we all knew that his greatest hope had been to turn Chang from his terrible course, and somehow save him.

"Thank you, gentlemen," he replied, choking back the tears, "you have proven yourselves true friends of Ming."

Not wanting him to be embarrassed by his display of emotion, Holmes was quick to lighten the conversation.

"How much longer will you be staying with us, my friend?"

"My sons and I are leaving for China tomorrow," he told us. "We have been too long away from our family. But now we may return and live in peace."

"We will miss you and your sons," I said sincerely.

"Thank you again, Doctor Watson. We shall miss you also."

At that moment the large double doors of the sitting-room opened, and in came our beloved Victoria with Emily and her son at her side. The Queen was stunning in full royal vestment, while Emily was a vision of loveliness in a dazzling gown of white and blue lace. Young Jeffry was also quite proper, but tugged at his tight collar continually, as one might expect of any small lad.

"Good evening, Your Majesty, Miss Cantaville," Charlie said as he greeted them.

"A fine good evening," Atkins echoed.

With that, the Queen gave them a warm smile and then brought Emily over to us.

"I wish to ask you gentlemen to escort Miss Cantaville and her son into the dining hall this evening," she began. "But be sure to give so wealthy a woman the proper respect." And then she winked.

"You may rest assured," Holmes told her with a wink of his own, "that proper care will be taken."

Emily then turned to me and hugged my neck.

"Oh, John," she whispered with excitement, "you won't believe how much she has gotten for Jeffry and me."

Our grand lady then met the Prime Minister in front of the doorway leading to the dining hall and bade us join them.

As we gathered round, the Queen suddenly turned and looked upon us with deep, caring eyes. And then she spoke.

"My friends, all of England shall be forever indebted to you. And while no words could ever express the gratitude that I personally feel at this moment, I want you to know that your

Queen shall never forget what you have done for her, and that, so long as I live, no request that you should make of me will ever fall upon a deaf ear. You will excuse me now if I show but a small favoritism. But I wish to say a special thank you to the man who gave me hope when there was no hope; a reason to go on when there was no reason. I speak now, not only as your Queen, but as a citizen of London, of England, and the world. I speak for all the men, women and children of our city. And I believe I speak for everyone here present when I say, thank you. Thank you, Sir Sherlock Holmes."

And then, as my shy associate stood red-faced and speechless, she came forward and kissed his cheek while we all broke into rousing applause.

* * * * *

ABOUT THE AUTHOR

Having lived in small towns all my life may seem dull to some, but I have found it a rich and rewarding existence. The middle child of thirteen children, I was fortunate enough to be raised in what I would call an, almost, Walton-like atmosphere of family joys and sorrows, triumphs and tragedies.

Remarkably, we are all still alive, except for my mother who lost her life to cancer at the early age of forty nine. But my father continued with remarkable courage--to say the least--and brought us all to adulthood.

I am forty seven now, and enjoy the memories of lazy nights in St. Henry; strumming my guitar on the front porch and singing songs with family and friends. I play guitar and piano and write songs and poems as well. I like telling stories, as I have been surrounded by family story tellers all my life. Always, my father, brothers and sisters, aunts and uncles and many family members, they tell the stories of the family's past whenever we come together.

I work with mentally and physically challenged adults, and have for eighteen years. I now live in the small town of Minster, Ohio with my wife and two teenage children. And as I do, the adventure of my life continues.